GUILTY AS SIN

ADAM CROFT

GET MORE OF MY BOOKS FREE!

To say thank you for buying this book, I'd like to invite you to my exclusive *VIP Club*, and give you some of my books and short stories for FREE.

To join the club, head to adamcroft.net/vip-club and two free books will be sent to you straight away! And the best thing is it won't cost you a penny — ever.

Adam Croft

For more information, visit my website: adamcroft.net

BOOKS IN THIS SERIES

To find out more about this series and others, please head to adamcroft.net/list.

It was the last day of Danielle Levy's life.

As she sauntered round the corner into Heathcote Road on her way back from a hard half-day's work at sixth-form college, she was glad that it hadn't been a full day and that she could enjoy the afternoon in the sun.

It had been Maths today. It was always bloody Maths. Despite the fact that she had chosen to study Drama and English Literature as her two main A-levels, her mother had insisted that she choose at least one 'proper' subject. She'd thrown in Classics as her fourth option. Another protest to piss her parents off, but she was actually quite enjoying it. She hoped one day to be a Drama teacher, or perhaps English. She'd be one of those cool teachers that all the kids loved, not like those stuffy idiots at Woodlands.

Woodlands was all right, she supposed. It wasn't an all-purpose college like the one she had planned to attend before her family moved to Mildenheath, but it was all right. The sixth-form college was somewhat amalgamated with the upper school, which ruined the sense of adult independence as far as she was concerned. How could you feel like you were no longer at school when you were in a school? The same teachers, the same classrooms. The same snotty-nosed little brats who didn't know what it meant to be grown up. She'd have to deal with that when she was a teacher, but she'd find a way.

Every day when she turned the corner into Heathcote Road, her heart sank a little. True enough, it was the road she lived on, but her house was a good seven hundred yards further along the road; a road which seemed to get longer and longer every time she walked it. She had lived at 101 Heathcote Road only for a couple of months, but she had already become attached to the house. It was on a quiet estate on the edge of town, mostly three- and four-bedroom houses, nice spacious gardens and no problems to worry about. Not like the last house. Passing the parade of shops, walking up the hill and exiting the right-hand bend to see her house standing proud in the summer sunshine always made her feel warm and glorious. It was home.

Darren's van was parked jauntily on the cracked concrete driveway as she skirted around the edge of the lawn towards the front door. Her step-father tended to finish work early on Fridays. Not that he didn't finish early on every other day. She guessed there wasn't much call for carpet fitters after 2pm on a weekday.

Turning her key in the lock and crunching the bottom of the door over the pile of letters which lay in wait on the doormat, she heaved her rucksack against the wine rack, picked up the post and made her way towards the kitchen. The door had been locked, so it was clear to Danielle that she was alone in the house. No biggie, though. It was a Friday and Darren often brought his van home and went straight to the pub after work on Fridays. A few hours of afternoon sun in the beer garden. Who could blame him?

It was then that she heard the familiar creaking of the back door.

It was dark. It might have been the middle of the day, but it was always dark here. The noise of the traffic outside had disappeared. The birds had stopped singing. Her chest had stopped heaving. His worries were gone.

He stood over her naked, quivering body as the last lights of consciousness began to ebb away from her battered shell. The odd low murmur escaped from her bruised and bloodied lips as the blood in her veins thickened and began to resist its final circuit. Her eyes rolled in her head, turning milky as he smirked, before jerking his head back and propelling a globule of spittle at her, watching it hit her eyeball and cascade down her lacerated cheek. Good shot.

She would be no bother any more. She was too close to the truth. Far too close. Her idle threats had pushed him over the line. There was no way she could have been allowed to live. Not with what she knew. He wouldn't do second-best, and certainly not to her. She thought she held the cards, but she was wrong. Now, as her life slowly slipped away from her, he hoped that she knew it. He was sure she did. He felt joyous, powerful at the act that he had committed. He felt good.

The sirens that bellowed and swirled as they raced past on their way to another emergency, completely unaware of the scene they'd just driven past, served only to reinforce his feeling that he was above the law. He was the law. The law had won.

He stepped backwards over the concrete floor and felt for the wooden handle. Jerking his hand upwards, he lifted the sledgehammer from the floor with a deep scraping on the rough concrete below. With a wry smile, he lifted it up above his head and brought it crashing down on her skull.

DS Wendy Knight stood slouched against the wall of the lift as it rose towards the third floor. Two weeks off work and she was knackered within a further two. *If you rest, you rust,* she remembered an old American actress once saying. Wendy certainly felt rusted up right now.

The juddering and shunting of the lift upon reaching the third floor almost knocked Wendy to her knees. As if simply confirming the arrival at the third floor for those who were still conscious, the lift bell pinged before the doors slid open and the familiar sight of Mildenheath CID greeted her. Another Monday morning.

Making her way towards her desk, she noticed that it had once again been used as a dumping ground for empty coffee cups and sandwich wrappers. One weekend off duty and your desk becomes a landfill site. The joys of life in Mildenheath CID. Casually stuck to the uppermost coffee cup was a gleaming yellow post-it note adorned with DCI Jack Culverhouse's distinctive handwriting.

Briefing – mispers – 9am

Short and sweet; that was Culverhouse's style. No wasted energy, no wasted time. Wendy smiled inside at the second word. It was a while since they'd had a missing persons case to deal with. Almost 200,000 people were reported missing in the UK every year, with three quarters of people being found within 48 hours and less than one percent of missing people being found dead. That was still a lot of people — almost 2,000, five a day — but the odds on dealing with a dead body were significantly lower than in a cut-and-dried murder case, where you were assured of dealing with the grim and grisly process of an horrific death.

Death terrified Wendy. It was an occupational hazard, but one she would rather avoid. She was petrified of her own death and truly hated having to deal with death as part of her job. Death could wait, though. She had other matters of life on her mind.

Deciding against having a coffee due to a lack of

cups with most of them piled up on her desk, Wendy picked up her Moleskine notebook and rounded the corner towards the briefing room, where she found the room scattered with her colleagues, all looking far more refreshed than she felt on this Monday morning. Luke Baxter, newly promoted Detective Sergeant, was sat in the front row against the window, sharing a joke with Culverhouse. Baxter's fast-tracked promotion still rankled Wendy. She knew the golden boy of Milden-heath CID was far less than he was cracked up to be. Unfortunately, Culverhouse saw things very differently. Nothing new there, then.

With a cough, Culverhouse rose and stepped slowly and purposefully in front of the information board as he waited for silence.

'Right. A nice little missing persons enquiry to kick us off this morning. Hopefully we can have the bird found by lunchtime and crack open a few tinnies.'

Culverhouse's comment was met with muted laughter from the men and rolled eyes from the women. He jabbed a finger at the blown-up photograph stuck to the information board. It showed a happy, smiling young woman posing in front of a Christmas tree in a delight-fully bad festive jumper. Wendy had noticed the growing trend in un-trendy clothing and admired the irony which had permeated fashion in recent years.

'Danielle Levy, aged seventeen. She was last seen attending sixth-form lessons at Woodlands on Friday lunchtime. Her mother and step-father said she didn't return home that afternoon as they had expected her to. She often went into town with friends during the afternoon when she didn't have any lessons, so they didn't worry at first but began to panic when she hadn't returned home that evening. She was officially reported missing late last night.'

Wendy nodded slowly as she jotted down the relevant notes in her notebook. A fairly routine case. Seventeen-year-old girls went missing all the time and were by far the most likely people to do so. She knew, however, that once the first couple of days had passed, the chances of finding a missing girl alive would slowly crumble. Danielle had already been gone for more than two days.

'DS Wing, I want you to get on to her mobile phone company and get some details on her most recent location. Baxter, I want you to man the phones at this end and get on to the local media and get some publicity on this. Frank, you and Debbie can start conducting door-to-door enquiries. See if the neighbours have seen her or if there's been any sign of a disturbance or argument recently. Knight, you're coming with me to speak to the parents.'

Wendy actually quite enjoyed being at Culverhouse's side when he carried out interviews and spoke with families. She saw herself as the yin to his yang, the good cop to his bad cop, and she was sure he realised this and appreciated it. Below the appreciation, though, was the realisation that as every minute and every second ticked by, the likelihood of finding Danielle Levy alive was rapidly diminishing.

4

Danielle Levy's house was situated a mile and a half south of the police station in Mildenheath, a tired-looking lamp-post the only eyesore on a row of houses sporting downstairs bay windows and oak trees to the front and rear. The lawn was neatly tended to — something Wendy would not have noticed before she had a lawn of her own, but which she now appreciated.

Culverhouse pressed the doorbell, shuffled his feet and cleared his throat. Wendy raised an eyebrow in warning that Culverhouse should exercise some tact.

The man who opened the door looked as though he was in his mid-thirties, although small flecks of grey hairs in his closely-cropped black cut belied his true age.

'Mr Levy?'

'Parker. Darren Parker. Danielle's mum and I aren't

married. You must be the two detectives. Please, come in.'

The white, glass-paned front door led into an open hallway. The staircase rose up the left-hand wall away from the door and the kitchen door was open at the far end of the hall. Darren Parker led Wendy and Culverhouse to the right-hand door and into the living room. Wendy took a seat by the bay window, Culverhouse preferring to stride around the living room inspecting ornaments and greetings cards as he began to speak to Darren.

'Someone had a birthday?'

'Danielle. Her seventeenth. Last month, actually, but we tend to keep the cards up until we get sick of the sight of them. Not much else to look forward to apart from Christmases and birthdays these days, is there?'

Culverhouse emitted a non-committal murmur. '"From your mum and step-dad" it says. I thought you weren't married?'

'We're not, but Danielle always calls me her step-father. Me and Miriam are as good as married anyway, so what's in a name?'

Wendy smiled. It had been a long time since she had heard the words of a truly caring father. 'So, when did you last see Danielle?' she said.

'In the morning before she went to school. Only

briefly. We said good morning at the top of the stairs as I went to work.'

'You're a carpet fitter, aren't you? Is that your van on the drive?'

'That's the one. Got my own business.'

'I see. And was there any sign that Danielle had been home at all on Friday after she finished at college?'

'Well, her rucksack was in the hall, so she must have been home. I think she said she had lessons up until lunchtime, though. I got back from work around one o'clock and her rucksack wasn't there then. I went out to walk the dog over Mildenheath Common for an hour or two and when I got back it was there, so she must have come back in between. Odd thing is, her shoes weren't there so I can only imagine she must have dropped her bag off and gone out somewhere."

'Can you think of anywhere she might have gone? A friend's house?' Wendy asked.

'We've tried all those. Danielle was always very streetwise and told us all her friends' names and phone numbers. We've spent the last day or two phoning round. We've even been up to the hospital to see if any unknown people have been admitted. We've just drawn an absolute blank. In retrospect, we probably should have phoned the police earlier, but we were so sure she had just gone into town or round to a friend's house. You hear it all the time, don't you? People going missing and then turning up because the parents have panicked too early. I guess... Well, you never think it's going to happen to you, do you?'

'I'm sure she'll be found safe and sound, Mr Parker,' Wendy said. Deep inside, she knew that the chances of this were fast diminishing. 'Are you sure that you and Mrs Levy don't know of anywhere else Danielle might have gone to?'

Darren shoved his hands in his jeans pockets and thought for a moment. 'I'm pretty sure, yes. We've gone through the list a hundred times. Miriam's out now, walking the dogs on the Common in some sort of vain hope of finding something.'

'You can leave the searching to us, Mr Parker,' Culverhouse said. 'I'm sure we'll find her soon. Do you mind if we have a quick look around her bedroom? Standard practice for a missing person.'

'Yes, of course. It's the first room on the right.'

Wendy and Culverhouse ascended the stairs and passed the bathroom door at the top before opening the door into Danielle's room. The door creaked slightly as it opened, revealing a room which looked remarkably like any other seventeen-year-old girl's room. It had the air of youth and innocence, but without the mess and untidiness of the early adolescent. The posters of pop stars and male idols were gone, replaced with newspaper cuttings of drama productions and photographs of shows she had appeared in. Wendy recognised Danielle in a few of the photographs. She looked happy, carefree.

Her wardrobe contained the usual fare for a seventeen-year-old girl: jeans, short skirts, party dresses and low-cut tops along with an assortment of coats, shoes and handbags. Danielle Levy was clearly a girl who cared about her appearance; an effort which her photographs showed to be every bit a success. Nothing seemed to be missing or out of place. Except for Danielle herself.

The stairs creaking underfoot on his descent, Culverhouse began to ask the question before he was even visible to Darren Parker.

'Do you know whether Danielle had a boyfriend at all?'

'Not as far as I know, no. She was quite open with us as her parents, but you know what young girls are like. I don't imagine for one minute she always told us everything.'

'Do you think her friends might have a better idea?'

'Quite possibly. I should imagine she'd have told at least one of them if she was involved with someone. I did ask them all when we phoned around, if any of them knew of a boyfriend or someone she might have gone to see.'

'And?'

'No-one knew of anyone. We really don't know who else she could be with. It's as if she's just vanished into thin air.'

'And there were no signs of a break-in at all?' Wendy asked.

'No, but then again... Oh, this is going to sound so stupid.'

'Go on, Mr Parker,' Culverhouse said calmly.

'Well, when I came home from walking the dogs the back door was unlocked. We usually lock it, and I know it was locked when I left for work in the morning as I hadn't unlocked it from the night before. I mean, it'd be pretty difficult for someone to get in that way, but not entirely impossible.'

5

Wendy sat lifeless at her desk, nursing an increasingly colder mug of coffee. Her lips were pursed, blowing away steam which no longer existed.

'You trying to make an ice lolly?' DS Steve Wing said.

'Hmmm? Oh, sorry. Lost in thought.'

'I'd noticed. You've been blowing on that coffee for the past twenty minutes. Not like your usual asbestos-tongued self,' he joked. Steve tended to be the one to inject humour into the incident room at Mildenheath CID and Wendy was often jealous of the way in which he was able to detach himself from situations and continue to function without all of the mental baggage that came with dealing with dead bodies and victims of serious crime.

'Yeah, just got a lot of stuff on my mind at the moment,' she said. 'Long days and short nights, you know how it is.'

'I don't think any of us really know how it is, Wendy. Not with what you've been through. You should probably have taken longer off work, no matter what Culverhouse says.'

'It wasn't down to Culverhouse. It was down to me. As he said, he would have had me in the next day if he could. A fortnight off was most definitely my idea, believe me.'

'True. Two weeks is maternity leave to him. Anyway, we've got an afternoon briefing at half-past. More news on the mobile phone records and door-to-door enquiries on the Danielle Levy case.'

'Mmmhmm. Any luck?'

'That's what the briefing's for,' Steve said with a smile.

'Yeah...' Wendy trailed off.

'Listen, Wendy, are you sure you're all right? I mean, I can always have a word with Culverhouse if you'd rather take more time off or have a break or something. Actually, scrap that. I'll speak to the Chief Constable. Hawes would shit himself if he thought there was a chance of you going mental and bringing some sort of court case against the force.'

'Nah, I'm fine. Honestly. Half past, yeah?'

As Wendy got up and left the room, Steve Wing gave it a minute or so before knocking on Culverhouse's door.

* * *

The morning briefing passed in a haze for Wendy as Culverhouse updated the team with the latest developments.

'Steve, what's the latest on the mobile phone records?' he said, addressing DS Wing.

'I got on to her network operator this morning, guv. Fortunately for us, she has an iPhone. Quite a recent model, and as she was in a built-up area the phone was sending broadcast signals every five or ten minutes. It was last picked up by three base station towers at 1.15pm, and using triangulation they were able to narrow it down to an area of about two hundred and fifty metres. That area pretty much centres on her house.'

'So she was at home when her mobile was last active?'

'Or near enough to it, yes. They could have been even more specific but it looks as though she had her phone's GPS function turned off, so they could only go by the mobile signal from the base stations. It's quite possible that she switched her phone off when she got home, or that it ran out of battery, or even that she left it at home. The thing is, the signal stops there. It doesn't mean she didn't leave the house, though. Just that her phone was either switched off or never left the house with her.'

'That could be about right, as her parents said her shoes weren't anywhere to be found in the house, so I think its looking likely that she left the house of her own accord. Or before she had a chance to take her shoes off, anyway.'

'Do you think there was an abduction, guv?' DS Frank Vine asked.

'It's possible, but I can't see a reason why at the moment. The step-father said the back door was left on the catch, whereas it's usually deadlocked. He says he locked it the night before and that it was unlocked when he came in from walking the dog on Friday afternoon.'

'So Danielle went out through the back door, then?'

'Or someone came in through it.'

Wendy hadn't been drinking heavily recently, she told herself. She'd been drinking just enough. What else can you do when you find out your own brother is a crazed killer, having murdered five women, your lover and tried to murder you?

She had cried all the tears she could cry in the last six weeks. Now, she felt almost no pain at all; it had been replaced with a feeling of complete numbness. Red wine helped numb what pain was left. She knew that Michael's court date later in the year would open up the wounds once again, but for now she was happy to feel nothing. She didn't know how she'd be able to face Michael in court, but she knew she had to. After he'd confessed everything to her, she knew she had to take to the witness stand when his court date came up.

She'd not yet had time to grieve for Robert, Michael's last victim and the man who she'd loved and her own brother had tried to set up as the serial killer. That had made things a hundred times worse. Anger and disbelief kept her grief for Robert under a watertight lid. For now, at least.

In those six weeks she had left her rented place and moved into a small house in a quiet residential area of Mildenheath, not far from the home of Danielle Levy. Her new one-bedroom mews house in Archer's Close was certainly cosy, as the estate agent had described it. Wendy hesitated to use the word 'cramped' as it was certainly spacious when compared to the space she had moved out of. What's more, she owned this place and could call it her own. Most importantly of all, though, the new house didn't hold the bad memories the old one did. She had her creature comforts here: a cul-de-sac location, a front lawn and enough space for her to spend her days away from the office.

Wendy stared at the box and ran her fingers over the raised lettering as she took another mouthful of wine. She was sure it wouldn't be necessary — it couldn't be necessary — but she was better safe than sorry. Putting the glass of wine down on the coffee table, she took the box into the bathroom and closed the door.

Emerging minutes later, Wendy picked the wine glass up from the coffee table and emptied its contents into the sink.

Wendy was glad that the brief greetings and conversations hadn't got past 'hello' and on to 'how are you?' that Tuesday morning as she wasn't entirely sure what her answer would be. She felt very little, caught somewhere between happiness, despair, joy and desperation.

Her state of mind was helped little by a particularly energetic and brash DCI Culverhouse who was now sauntering over towards her desk.

'Knight. Your arse, my office, now.'

Not one to turn down a polite request, Wendy rose from her chair and followed Culverhouse into his office. The door closed with a click and Culverhouse turned and perched himself on the edge of his desk.

'Oh, you brought the rest of you too. Never mind.'

'You wanted to see me, guv,' Wendy said, ignoring his attempts at a joke.

'I did. Steve said you were a bit down in the dumps.'

'He *what*?' she said in disbelief. 'I'm fine, guv, really.'

'No, I mean what I'm saying is you're probably likely to be a bit mardy, aren't you?'

'What? Why?'

'Well, the Michael stuff.'

'Are you trying to tell me that, as a kind and caring man, you completely understand that I might be psychologically affected by the fact that my brother turned out to be a serial killer, murdered my boyfriend and then tried to kill me?'

'I wouldn't have put it in quite such a poofy way, no.'

'Well I'm not. I'm fine.'

'You might think so, but no-one else does, Knight. Listen, I've booked you in to speak to that shrink in Counselling. Maybe she can help you sort your head out a bit.'

'My head doesn't need sorting out, guv. I just want to get on with my work.'

'Well you're not doing much work sat there staring into space and taking evenings off, are you?'

'I've had other stuff on my mind,' Wendy said, averting her eyes.

'Other than a homicidal brother and a brutally

murdered ex-partner? Your mind works wonders sometimes, Knight.'

Wendy sighed. She knew she was going to have to
tell him. It would probably make matters worse, but she
didn't have much choice.

She sighed.

'I'm pregnant.'

It never got dark in Mildenheath. Not really. Even the darkest, dankest alleyways glowed with the light pollution caused by this sprawling urban town, darkened only by the smog and traffic fumes. It meant that you could never hide in Mildenheath. Not unless you knew where you were and what you were doing. He wished it could be darker right now, but this would have to do. He didn't have much choice. It was almost time.

It was a nice coincidence that he was stood here, at the end of Corpse Walk. Legend had it that the alleyway got its name due to its previous use as the main walkway for coffins to be carried through from the residential areas to the town church for funeral services. The church had been built in 1132, and Corpse Walk can't have been much younger. Nowadays it was sat just off the crossroads in the centre of Mildenheath, looking down over the smog and traffic. Just yards from the bustling main road, the juxtaposition between urbanity and legend, between the past and the future, between life and death, sat perfectly with him.

He could hear a car stopped at the traffic lights at the other end of the alleyway, the engine idling, its owner hell-bent on letting everyone else listen to his shitty dub-step music. What was it with the idiots in this town? He could barely hear himself think, let alone hear the footsteps as they came towards him. He flicked his head around the edge of the wall and glanced down the tunnel. His man was only feet away. It was time.

Readjusting his grip on the now-sweaty hard wood of the baseball bat, he lifted it up onto his right shoulder as if ready to receive a perfect pitch.

He fixed his eyes on the wall opposite, waiting for the man's shadow to appear. After what seemed like an age, the bobbing shadow of the man's head came into view, elongated by the street light at the far end of Corpse Walk. Three seconds. Two seconds. One. He swung.

Home run.

'Pregnant? Well how did that happen?'

'Do you want a diagram, guv?'

'Don't be cocky. I mean... what, Ludford?'

'Yes, Ludford.' Her face fell now as she contemplated bringing a baby into the world. A baby without a father. A baby whose father had been murdered and mutilated by its own uncle. Born to a mother who wasn't ready, a mother who could barely look after herself right now. A tear rolled down her cheek.

'Well, are you happy or not?' Culverhouse asked, not quite sure what to say. It wasn't often Culverhouse was lost for words.

'What does it look like, guv?'

'I don't know, do I? You birds are always crying whether you're happy or sad.'

'I really have no idea. I mean, of course I'm happy, but I'm scared as well. I never planned for this to happen. In a way, I don't want it to happen.'

'What, you mean you're going to, like... Culverhouse made a jabbing and twisting motion with his hand.

'No! Besides, I think they tend to give you a pill these days. It's not the sixteenth century, no matter how much you like to think it is. Anyway, how could I abort it? It's the last living part of Robert. I couldn't do that, guv. How could I? I was up all night thinking about it and I've come to the conclusion that I can't kill Robert all over again. I'm going to have the baby.'

Culverhouse was silent for a few moments as he tried to digest the information.

'I suppose you'll be leaving me to bugger off on maternity leave now, then.'

'Not seven weeks into my pregnancy, I'm not, no. In fact, I doubt I'll have much time off at all, if any. Moping about at home isn't exactly my idea of fun right now. I'd much rather keep busy if that's all right with you, guv.'

'I admire your spirit, Knight, but even I know that's not sensible. You're probably entitled to a few months, but I'd have to check with the Pushchairs & Placentas department. Now, about that counselling malarkey. I've spoken to the shrink and she reckons she can see you tomorrow morning. No ifs, no buts. I want you to go along, if only to stop you crying all over my bloody paperwork for a couple of hours.'

Wendy let out a relieved laugh through her tears. 'OK, but only to save your paperwork. But I don't want to use the police counsellors, though. That would be a bit too close to home. It would be like having to tell my deepest, darkest secrets to you. No offence.'

'None taken. Perish the thought. I know far too much already. Now, go on, get out. Both of you.'

Wendy smiled.

It was another dark, dank Wednesday morning for Donald Radley. Sure, the sun was shining and the birds were singing but it was dark and dank all the same as far as he was concerned. Business had not been good, not in a long time. The recession had bitten hard, and it hurt. If only his stupid fucking wife hadn't spent so much money on shoes and spa treatments, maybe they might be able to rein in the spending and keep their heads above water. No chance of that happening now. He was in way over his head.

He'd already remortgaged the house twice and the small salary he paid himself was just about covering his credit card repayments each month. He'd tried everything to keep it down: balance transfers, 0% deals, offsetting equity. Whatever he did, the debt just kept on growing.

He felt the bile rise from the pit of his stomach as he drove down St David's Way and pulled up outside Unit 5. It was like waking up in the morning to see the one thing that had taken everything good out of his life. A building, a shell. A destroyer.

He sat in the car for a few minutes longer, summoning up the courage to face another day of red-letter bills and bulging overdrafts. The fact was, nobody wanted stationery nowadays. People could print their own letterheads and get business cards made up for next to nothing on the internet. Ah, the internet. Radley Stationery had been a little slow on the uptake when it came to the internet. Not on Donald's part, though; that slimy, good-for-nothing business partner of his had decreed that the world wide web was nothing more than a passing fad and an expensive one at that. No need for a website. No need to sell online. It wouldn't last. People would always prefer bricks and mortar, and the internet would be expensive. Yeah, it had proved to be expensive, all right. Fucking expensive.

Bad things always happened to good people. He knew that. He felt stupid and foolish at the time, effort and money he had pumped into this place, only to be taken for a ride. Bob Arthurs epitomised the definition of a silent partner. Silent except when he disagreed with something Donald wanted to do. Which was everything. He barely set foot in the unit, but he still felt the need to stick his fucking oar in everywhere he could.

As far as Bob Arthurs was concerned, he'd put his money in as an investment and he wanted to make sure he was going to be able to get it back out again when he wanted to. Fat chance of that happening. He couldn't have had a fiver from the till if he wanted to, because it wasn't there.

Donald didn't know who he hated the most: Bob Arthurs for constantly getting in his way and driving the business into the ground, his wife for spending the money they didn't have, or himself for trusting either of these two witless idiots.

He thumped the dashboard and unlocked his car. He breathed in deeply and quickly, and out slowly. He felt like he was about to walk out on stage in front of ten thousand people. Hell, that would've been easier than having to spend another day in this place.

Of all the horrors he had expected to await him inside, he was not expecting this one.

She hated him. She truly, truly hated him. On paper, it came without rhyme or reason but she was sure that she was right. She was always right. After all, these things just built up, didn't they? The anger, the frustration, the all-consuming contempt. She knew that she had done the right thing.

It had been on her mind ever since. Her counsellor had told her that it was because she wouldn't let the past go, because she kept thinking about it and mulling it over in her mind. She didn't agree. As far as she was concerned, the more she thought about it the more she realised what she had put up with for all those years. The more she realised, the more she hated him.

It was an odd sort of hatred. It almost bordered on pity. She recalled the excitement building up inside her.

The nerves. The trepidation. As she sat and stared at the photograph, the thoughts and feelings came flooding back. Humiliation, shame, and unrelenting anger. She had used those feelings to her advantage, though. Now, not only was she on top of him, but she was on top of the world. She was free. Free from what, she did not know, but she was free. She was also alone.

It had been a long time coming, but she still didn't regret a moment of it. Knowing the pain he had gone through as a result of what she'd done had brought nothing but joy to her. But she knew it could not last. The joy was slowly getting weaker and the pain of what had come before was growing more distant. Surely even he must have learnt his lesson by now. Even the most pig-headed arrogant man on earth must have learnt. Even the biggest sinners could be redeemed, and she hoped that now things had evened out.

She knew one day she would have to face the music. She knew that day would be soon.

12

Culverhouse breathed heavily as he approached the door of Unit 5, St David's Way. If what he had been told was correct, he knew he wouldn't be taking too many deep breaths once he was inside. The thick D-shaped Formica handle was cold to the touch, the draft excluder whooshing and squeaking slightly against the floor tiles as the door opened.

It was the smell. Always the smell. It never left you once you'd smelt it. Often, when he was lying in the bath or sitting at his kitchen table, he'd breathe in and would still smell it. It stuck in your nostrils forever. You got a nose for a dead body after a while, and this one smelt very dead indeed.

'Knight, wait outside for the pathologist. He shouldn't be far behind,' Culverhouse said, trying hard to breathe in through his nose and not his mouth. He didn't want to have to taste it as well as smell it.

Wendy was only too pleased to acquiesce. She'd also seen and smelt her fair share of dead bodies and wasn't particularly keen to be the first person inside.

Culverhouse decided against getting too close; he could see plenty from here. He could see the tops of the feet, the skin bubbled and blistered around the edges of the cavernous openings which revealed every individual metatarsal and a distinct lack of flesh. A chemical smell hung in the air, barely masking the odour of the decomposing body itself. The eye sockets had peeled back, revealing the deep smoked-salmon-coloured flesh and remnants of what was once an eyeball. The hair was non-existent; most of the scalp had burnt through to sheer white bone.

'Looks like an acid job, sir,' the young constable said. He'd been the first on the scene and, despite his youthful innocence, seemed far less bothered by the mutilated body than Culverhouse.

'Hydrochloric,' Culverhouse added.

'You can tell?'

'Yeah, it's a hobby of mine, you great berk. Of course you can tell. I've seen plenty of bodies in my time, Constable.'

'Do you reckon it might be our missing girl?' he

asked, showing an interest in the goings on at CID, keen to impress his superiors.

'How the fuck do I know? Silly me, I didn't think of commissioning an e-fit of what she might look like with half her fucking face melted off. Hopefully the patholo-gist won't be long and he'll be able to tell us for sure. Who found it?'

'The owner of the business, sir. A Mr Donald Radley.'

'Any sign of forced entry to the unit?'

'He says not. Everything was locked up as it was left. No broken windows, and the alarm wasn't activated.'

'Who else could have had a key or access to the alarm?'

'Any of the senior staff, conceivably. There's a front door with the alarm system wired up to it, and only one door at the back. That's got a commercial recycling bin jammed up against it and that hasn't been moved in a while. Took us ages to get the thing open, so there's no way anyone's been through there recently.'

'Nice little fire hazard,' Culverhouse said.

Janet Grey, the pathologist, entered the room, her high heels clip-clopping on the stone floor of the ware-house. 'DCI Culverhouse. Always a pleasure,' Grey said sarcastically.

'Janet.'

'So, how long's the body been here?'

'No idea. The owner says it definitely wasn't here last night,' Culverhouse said.

'He's sure about that?'

'I think it's safe to say he'd probably notice, Janet.'

'Only asking. You'd be surprised what the eye misses.'

'Quite possibly so, but I don't imagine his bleedin' nose would've.'

Janet Grey was, by now, far more interested in the body than in conversation with Culverhouse. Culverhouse always admired anyone who took a real interest in their job and had a passion for their work, but it disturbed him slightly that her face seemed to light up every time she attended a suspicious death.

'Mmm, interesting,' she said. 'Blunt trauma to the front of the face and ligature marks around the neck. Probably from a pair of hands, I'd say. Fortunately the acid didn't take out too much of the neck tissue. It's mostly the head, hands and feet. I'm no psychologist or profiler, Jack, but I'd say this is something to do with identity.'

'What, that the killer didn't want the person identified?'

'Oh, no, I doubt that. We can always identify a body. Certainly one with far less left of it than this. We've got dental records, DNA, all sorts. What I mean is that I'd suggest the killing was motivated by identity in some way. Getting rid of the face and extremities, including the fingers and fingerprints. It's a classic sign.'

'Beaten up, strangled and given an acid bath, though? Bit extreme, isn't it?'

'Depends how badly the killer wanted to get rid of him.'

'Him? You mean this isn't our missing girl?'

'Definitely not. Look at the hips. Far narrower than any woman I've ever known. Women have much wider, child-bearing hips. The shape of the skull gives it away, too, to the trained eye. I can't say for sure until I get it into the lab and on the table, but I'm willing to bet there's not a uterus in there, either.'

'So who's this then?'

'That's not for me to say, Jack, but it's not your missing girl.'

13

The waiting room at the counselling clinic was brightly lit but bitterly cold. A smell of antiseptic hung in the air; a smell only usually associated with hospitals and places meant to be kept clean. Brain antiseptic, Wendy thought. That's what I need. Clean it all out and start again.

The lady at the reception desk looked quite content to carry on with her task of writing letters to whomever she may be writing them, occasionally answering the phone in a manner far too jovial for her general demeanour. The people ringing here are likely to need a bit of cheering up, though, Wendy thought.

A series of posters adorned the wall, much as they did at any given medical institution across the country.

No signs of limp cigarettes and cancerous lungs here, though.

One in four people will experience a mental health problem.

Mental Health Awareness Week: Bipolar disorder causes severe mood swings that can leave a person feeling manic or depressed.

In every secondary school classroom there will be two young people who have self-harmed.

Depressing reading, not entirely conducive to cheering up their clients, Wendy thought.

The door in front of her clicked open and a dark-haired woman appeared in a white blouse and black trousers. Her black-rimmed glasses were perched on her nose as she smiled pleasingly, her eyes barely visible in the folds of her smile as she ushered out an Indian-looking woman and her child. The child looked no older than five or six, with medium-brown curly locks dancing over her head. Wendy watched them pass.

'Wendy Knight?' The woman was smiling again, and cocked her head to the side as if to welcome Wendy in. *Next, please.*

Wendy followed her into the room. Certificates were hung in a jovial and haphazard manner on the wall closest to the counsellor's desk, shelves presenting teddy bears and stuffed bunny rabbits, a corner displaying all manner of children's toys. The three armchairs and the wall of books reminded Wendy that this was a serious, adult place. At that moment, though, she might have been more contented in the toy corner. An escape away from the real world of computers and certificates.

Wendy sat down in one of the armchairs, as motioned by the counsellor.

'I'm Linda Street, and I'm a psychological counsellor. Now, I've read a few of your notes but first of all I'd just like you to tell me in your own words why you're here and what you hope to get out of these sessions.'

What did she hope to get out of these sessions? What did she hope to get out of anything? What use was hope?

'Well, I'm back at work after having four weeks off on compassionate leave. My last investigation was on the team investigating the Bowline Knot murders recently.'

'And the murderer turned out to be your brother, is that right?'

'Yes. He also killed my partner and tried to kill me, too.' Wendy spoke matter-of-factly as she relayed the bare essentials to Dr Street. Her voice gave away no emotion whatsoever. She had cried so much over the past six weeks that she had no more tears to shed. Just cold, hard facts.

'And how did that make you feel?'

Wendy snorted. 'How do you think it bloody made me feel?'

'I'd like you to tell me, Wendy. In your own words.'

Wendy thought for a moment, trying to make sense of her dulled emotions.

'Hurt. Used. Panicked. Dirty. Stupid. Foolish. Angry. Resentful. Devastated. Confused.'

'That's a lot of feelings.'

'It was a lot of drama.'

'And how does drama make you feel?' the psychologist asked.

What a bloody stupid question, Wendy thought. She hated drama. All she wanted was a quiet life. Granted, her career choice somewhat belied that fact, but she had never felt comfortable with confrontation. Unlike many of her colleagues, she was actually quite happy for her position to be slowly overtaken by a deluge of paperwork. As long as the criminals were stopped and put away, she was happy for that to happen in any way necessary. She certainly wasn't one of Culverhouse's ilk, constantly complaining about paperwork and political correctness.

'I don't like drama, on the whole.'

'And do you think that's conducive to your job?'

'I'm a good detective,' she said drily.

'I'm not disputing that, Wendy. I'm trying to find out whether your job might exacerbate your psychological state and cause you some problems which we'll need to iron out. Do you think you might need more time away to properly come to terms with what happened?'

'Iron out? My own brother framed my partner for a series of murders, killed him and then tried to kill me. Now I'm carrying a baby that has no father and a mother who doesn't know what to do,' Wendy said, her voice cracking.

'You're pregnant?'

'Yes. Only a few weeks. I must have been pregnant at the time of Robert's death.'

'I'd certainly reiterate what I just said, then, Wendy. Do you think it's wise to be back at work so soon, considering? A pregnancy can make your psychological state very delicate indeed, and I'm not sure the physical stress of your job is the best thing to subject an unborn baby to.'

Wendy almost laughed. 'That's out of the question.

I'm working on two very important cases right now. I promise you, if I sit at home and mope then I'll be a hundred times worse. Work is the only thing that keeps my mind busy and keeps me just the right side of sane. I don't want this baby turning out to be a crackpot as well.'

'I'm not suggesting that you stay at home and mope, Wendy. Just that you take the rest and recuperation time that you and your baby both need. Perhaps a holiday might do you some good. See some sights, have a change of scenery.'

'What my baby and I need is to try to forget what happened and move on. All I have is my work and I need to work to forget. Even with the reminders that come with the job, I can't just sit around and do nothing. The last four weeks have been hell for me. I have to keep busy.'

'I just think there are better ways for you to keep busy than to subject yourself to a high-stress job. I know you wanted to see somebody independent of work, but I know the police force offers a fantastic range of support for—'

'I don't want support!' Wendy shouted. 'I don't want help and I didn't even want to come to these fucking stupid counselling sessions, either. I don't want to talk about what happened. I just want to get on with my life.'

Within a minute, Wendy had left the clinic.

14

Janet Grey grinned masochistically as she tied her long blonde hair back into a bun, the hygienic cap sitting snugly over it. Culverhouse suspected that she got a kick out of seeing coppers baulk and retch at the sight and smell of a dissected cadaver. Pathologists got used to it eventually, but even the hardest and most experienced of coppers still had trouble. Pathologists could detach themselves from the body. They had facts, statistics and science. It was the family the coppers had to deal with. The friends of the deceased. A life and a death.

'So, as I was telling you at the scene of the crime, this is a male body, not a female. The fact that the skull contained three pounds of sawdust where the brain should be was the major give-away.' She shot a wry smile at Culverhouse.

'Very good, Miss Grey. And there was me thinking this pathology bollocks was a skilled profession.'

'Oh, it is. In fact, you'll be pleased to know that the real give-away was that his brain was actually larger than a woman's would be. Most men's brains are. We just use ours more effectively,' she added, before Culverhouse could speak.

'Is there anything we could use to try and identify the body? Dental records? You said it should be easy enough.'

'Oh, it should be. But there's not much left of the teeth, I'm afraid. They've been bashed around a fair bit.'

'What about DNA? Skin swabs? Hair follicles?'

'Nothing that matches the police database.'

'Great. So how the bloody hell are we meant to identify who he was?'

'Well, I can tell you, Jack. A Mr Robert Arthurs, of 9 Vicarage Road, Mildenheath. Born 16th July 1953. And an organ donor.'

'That's very precise.'

'Yes, well it does help when the deceased remembers to keep his driving licence in his wallet.' Janet Grey grinned as she held up the pristine pink card. 'Although, I would have thought you'd have checked that already.'

'Well, I must admit that when you've got a body with

half its face and flesh missing, you don't tend to expect to need to go hunting for his library card.'

'First rule of policing, DCI Culverhouse. Remember the basics!'

'Thank you, Doctor. I'll bear that in mind next time I'm telling you how to spend your day prodding dead bodies.'

Janet Grey smiled and ignored the comment. 'Your problem now, Jack, is to find out who Mr Arthurs was and why he was in the unit in the first place.'

'Well, presuming he's the same Bob Arthurs who was a partner in Radley Stationery, I don't think that will be too difficult.'

15

Darren Parker had to get out of the house, if only for an hour or two. The constant nervous waiting and anguish was too much. Would it look insensitive to go out for a drink or two? He told himself not. It would help him to cope.

He couldn't drink at his local, The Spitfire. One thing he didn't want was to get dragged into conversation with people who would only ask about Danielle and whether there had been any news. He could do without that for one night. He was going out to get away from the same thoughts that kept going through his mind.

The evening was warm, so he decided he'd head for the other side of Mildenheath. The George and Dragon. He'd not been there in a while. A few pints of bitter would slip down nicely, numb the pain. Plus he didn't know anyone in there so wouldn't have to worry about people going on and on about Danielle. In his heart of hearts, he knew that the inevitable phone call or visit from the police would come sooner or later. The thought of what he had to lose was unbearable. In his heart, Danielle was his.

He felt a drop of sweat running down his spinal recess, collecting in the waistband at the top of his shorts. Summer nights in Mildeneath were sometimes unbearably humid. The joys of living in a built-up area. An area where everyone knew everyone. An area where no secret was ever safe.

The welcoming noise of friendly chatter, barstools groaning on wooden floorboards and the smell of freshly-poured beer transformed the George and Dragon into a heavenly escape from the outside world. Pulling a barstool towards him, Darren ordered a pint of Sunshine Bitter and allowed himself to soak up the atmosphere and surroundings. He could forget the outside world for an hour or two. God would grant him that.

A man adjacent to Darren was excitedly telling his friend about his news of the day. 'I'm tellin' you, Pete. Absolutely mutilated. Ol' Mr Radley came in this mornin' and found 'im sat there in the middle of the ware'ouse. 'Arf 'is face missin', 'e reckons.'

'Shit. Sounds like a contract killing to me. Probably one of them gangs or something. Or he hadn't been paying his bills again.'

'Nah, you've been watchin' too many of them American films, aintcha? Not too far from the troof, though. See, a few boys down the ware'ouse reckon ol' Gary McCann might 'ave 'ad summink to do wiv it.' The man's eyes widened and his voice lowered as he spoke his name.

'Gary McCann? You're having a laugh. I thought he'd packed that game in long ago. He's too old for that bollocks.'

'Nah, not a chance. Only a couple of years ago 'e bumped off 'is wife, innit? Similar story, 'n all – baseball bat and an acid shower. Startin' to look a bit familiar, ain't it? Gotta admit.'

'Too right there, Tel. Nasty piece of work, that McCann. Coppers nicked him yet? Gotta be on their radar as a suspect, surely.'

'No chance! 'E's got more lives than a bleedin' cat! Bung a brief a few grand and he'd be off the hook in no time. Nah, I reckon they'll 'ave to 'ave somethin' pretty concrete on 'im before they can nick 'im.'

The man known as Pete nodded and drained his glass.

16

The manilla folder left DCI Culverhouse's hand and landed with a thwack on the wooden desk. Wendy watched with interest as he rubbed his chin and grimaced, the sound of his dry hand rasping against stubble.

'I knew it. I bloody well knew it.'

'Knew what, guv?' Wendy asked.

'This Radley warehouse murder. I thought it sounded a bit familiar. Baseball bat and hydrochloric acid. It matches the MO of another murder a couple of years back. One Tanya McCann.'

'Think I remember,' Wendy said. 'How can you be sure, though? Sounds a bit vague.'

'I'm sure, all right. Firstly, we don't exactly get many people subjected to having their faces caved in with baseball bats and hydrochloric acid dumped on them on a regular basis in Mildenheath. Secondly, there are just too many links. One big link, in particular. Gary McCann.'

'A relation?'

'Her husband. It was him who killed her. I mean, we were never able to get the evidence to convict him, but everyone knew it was him. He's a clever sod, that McCann, and we're not going to find it any easier this time, either. Slimier than a fucking eel.'

'But why would Gary McCann want to kill Bob Arthurs? What's the link? And why would he use the same method when he sailed so close to the wind last time?'

'To rub our fucking noses in it, Knight. That's what Gary McCann's like. A proper piece of work. Now, Bob Arthurs was a partner in Radley Stationery. Let's just say that where there's a struggling business in the town, Gary McCann usually creeps up sooner or later. And so do the profits of the companies.'

'You mean he's a loan shark?'

'A loan shark, a fraudster, a money launderer and a downright gangster, if you ask me. As I say, we've never been able to pin any of it on him. He's too clever. He has this horrible tendency of propping up failing businesses with private loans and using the companies to launder money. Rumour has it that he's got links with Moroccan drug cartels, but that's going to be even harder to prove. Wouldn't surprise me one bit, though.'

'If he's got that much behind him, I'm amazed we haven't been able to pin something on him yet, guv,' Wendy said, assuming that this gangster legend was probably as enormously over-embellished as most of the other ones she'd heard over the years.

'Like I said. He's a clever bugger. A very clever bugger.'

'And you think he might have killed Bob Arthurs over some sort of business deal?'

'Officially? It's too early to say. Between you and me? He's guilty as sin.'

Luke Baxter was whistling an irritating tune as he casually filed papers away in the filing cabinet. Wendy had never been particularly hot on music, but she was pretty sure that he wasn't whistling a real song. You just know when someone is whistling for the sake of it.

'Do you fancy doing something constructive, Luke?' Wendy asked.

'I'm a little busy right now, Wendy. Sorry. I might have some time free this afternoon, though,' he replied with a cocky smile.

'Oh, might you?' She turned to Frank Vine. 'In that case, Frank, could you pop over to see Bob Arthurs's family and try to find out what they know about a Gary McCann? We believe there may have been some business links. The family might not have been aware, but it's worth a shot.'

Baxter piped up again. 'No need, Frank. I've already done that this morning.' He smiled at Wendy.

She could feel the blood raging through her temples. 'You what?'

'I've already spoken to them. I had a tip-off that this chap McCann might have been involved so I went round and asked them on my way back here.'

'Luke, do you have any idea who this "chap McCann" is?'

'Yeah, a bit of a dodgy bloke, if you ask me.'

'Dodgy doesn't come near to it, Luke, from what I've heard. How dare you go off on a hunch behind everyone else's back?'

Baxter stayed silent, shuffling his feet uncomfortably. Frank Vine was the first to pipe up. 'Uh, it wasn't behind everyone's back. I knew.'

'You knew? So why did you say you'd go and speak to them again?'

'I didn't, actually.'

'Who else knew?' Wendy asked, addressing the rest

of the incident room. The assembled officers were now shuffling as uncomfortably as Luke Baxter. 'Right. So when I said you went behind everyone's back, you actually just went behind my back. Why didn't you tell me too, Luke?'

'You seemed busy.'

'I seemed busy? Of course I seemed fucking busy; I'm in the middle of a murder investigation!'

'All right, sorry.'

'Sorry? Is that it?'

'What else do you expect? I've apologised. Mistakes happen.'

'Luke, the biggest mistake that happened was you being promoted to DS. You're a smarmy, conniving little shit and treating your colleagues like dirt won't get you anywhere. Just stay out of my way.'

Wendy left the incident room and slammed the door behind her.

17

The Prince Albert was a popular jaunt for the local police force, situated, as it was, next door to Mildenheath Police Station on Westgate. It was fair to say that there was rarely any trouble at the Prince Albert. Culverhouse picked up his pint of bitter and led Wendy over to the corner table at the front window. Copper's seat, back to the window, of course. It was impossible to see anything through the frosted glass and net curtains, but it made Culverhouse feel safe and important. He was on watch.

Wendy sipped her orange juice delicately, as she always tried to do at first. After an evening sat talking to an increasingly inebriated Culverhouse, she knew she would progress on to larger and larger gulps.

She admired the genteel decoration of the pub, the

horse brass decorating the out-of-use fireplace and the quaint sets of pub games stacked up in the corner.

It was Culverhouse who spoke first. 'Baxter's had some good ideas and leads on the Danielle Levy case.'

'I bet he has,' Wendy said.

'Sorry, Knight. Can you sound a bit more jealous for me? I don't think I quite picked up on that.'

'I'm not jealous. I'm pissed off, if the truth be told.'

'With what? Baxter?'

'Yeah, Baxter. I appreciate his input, but I can't help feeling a bit... undermined at times.' A downright lie, and she knew it. She didn't appreciate his input. Not one iota. She thought he was an interfering little fuckwit and she would be glad to see him kicked off the case.

'He's not so bad. He needs to be eased in. He's a good copper.'

'Eased in? We've got a missing persons enquiry and a murder enquiry to deal with at the moment. How is that easing him in? He could be a liability, guv. He's barely out of uniform. Christ knows why he's been fast-tracked to DS.'

'Nonsense. I think he'll add a lot of value to the team.'

'He lowers the value, guv! He's done nothing but interfere with my leads and undermine me since he started on these cases. I don't want to give any ultima-tums, but I'm finding it bloody impossible to work with him.'

'Listen, Knight,' Culverhouse said, leaning in. 'Bax-ter's a promising young copper. All right, he might be a bit wet behind the ears but he's going to make a bloody good detective one day.'

'I doubt it.'

'I know it. I was once like that, Knight. The boy needs nurturing. He's a rough diamond.'

'Nurturing?' Wendy asked. 'What, so he can turn out like you?'

'Would that be such a bad thing?'

Wendy stayed quiet. Very quiet. Her raised eyebrow told Culverhouse all he needed to know to answer his question.

'Listen, Knight. The reason the powers-that-be don't like me is because I'm old school. All right, it might not be politically correct or any of that bullshit, but it works. I get results. That's why I'm still here. I was like Baxter once, a new copper full of ideas and aspirations to change the world. But the world can't be changed, Knight. It's a fucking shit world and it'll always be a fucking shit world. The best thing we can do is stamp on the shit. There aren't many coppers like me left, and when I'm gone, this police force will go to pot with red tape and political correctness. Don't get me wrong, but every police force needs a bit of the old school.'

'And you think that turning Baxter into a carbon copy of you is going to help the police force?' Wendy asked.

'He'll get results, like I get results. Listen. When I joined the force, the DI was a man called Jack Taylor. Now, he was really old school. The whole police force was compared to how it is now, but DI Taylor was a visionary, Knight. He could see the way things were going, the way we weren't able to nick the bastards because of red tape and warrants coming out of our ears. DI Taylor was a good man. One night, we'd gone round to speak to a bloke who'd been battering his wife. She was sat on the stairs sobbing, and wouldn't make a statement to us because she knew he'd get away with a ticking off and she'd be in for a right kicking when he got back home again. We couldn't touch him, despite the blood literally being on his hands. He let me get the first kick in, Taylor did. He stood there and watched as I beat that bastard to within an inch of his life. To this day, I still don't know why I did it, but I knew it was the right thing to do. You could see the pride on Taylor's face, knowing his legacy was in safe hands. And do you know what? That bloke never touched his wife again. Didn't dare. Because he'd had a proper punishment. Tell me that's what would happen if he went to court and got a fifty quid fine.'

'It doesn't mean that's the right way to go about things, guv.'

'Nonsense. Of course it's the right way to go about things. The woman called us because she wanted her husband to stop beating her up. We took action and he stopped beating her up. Job done. None of this namby-pamby political correctness bollocks. That wasn't the first or the last time, but I can tell you now that we got a result every single fucking time. She got hundreds of kickings before that, he got just one and the violence stopped. A means to an end, Knight.'

Wendy picked at her fingernails and changed the subject.

'What happened to DI Taylor?'

Culverhouse fell silent, his eyes drawn to the dregs in his pint glass. He ran his fingers through his hair and sighed.

'He's not around any more.'

'Retired?'

'In the passive sense. He went too far one day. Funny thing is, he wasn't even on duty. He was in a post office queue in Braylsford and some little shit tried to hold the place up with a gun. Local gang trying to make a name for themselves, trying to ruin what had been a nice quiet little market town. Taylor had seen more than enough of that shit in his time, so he stepped in. Wrestled the gun out of the kid's hand and elbowed him in the face. Knocked him clean out.' Culverhouse looked choked. He swallowed and continued to speak through a large sigh. 'The kid went down and hit his head on the counter. Died two days later from a brain haemorrhage.'

'What happened to Taylor?'

'He was given the option of resigning or being pushed. Stupid old sod was too proud for his own good and left them to sack him. Lost his wife and his house. All he ever had was the police force and when that was gone he lost everything. He always told me he'd die in his uniform, doing what he loved best for his country and his community. Fact is, he died face down in a gutter with a bottle of Jack Daniel's in his hand.' A single, solitary tear built up on Culverhouse's lower eyelid and began its journey down his cheek. 'And I will *never* forgive myself for not helping him, Knight. I will never let those bastards ruin our chances of getting real results. And if DS Baxter can take even 10% of that pride and belief with him in his career, I'll die a happy man.'

'That's why you're trying to fast-track him?'

'As best I can, yeah. The further up you get, the

harder it is for them to get rid of you. I should know. That's the only reason I'm still knocking about.' He let out a small laugh followed by a large sniff. Opening his mouth with a noise as if he'd just woken up, Culverhouse rubbed his red eyes and smiled at Wendy before finishing his beer.

18

Gary McCann's house sat proudly at the end of a sweeping driveway, nestled behind black wrought iron gates on Meadow Hill Lane. The road was often considered to be the comparative Millionaires' Row of Mildenheath, if there ever could be such a thing. The town hardly had its fair share of millionaires, but Meadow Hill Lane was the closest it was going to get.

DCI Culverhouse pulled off the road and came to a stop before the gates, noticing that Gary McCann's driveway was perfectly sizeable before you even got as far as the gate. He got out of the car and approached the barrier, pressing the brushed silver button on the intercom system.

'Yes?' said a voice a few seconds later.

'Mobile stripper for Mr McCann.'

'Ah, DCI Culverhouse. It's been too long.'

With that, the intercom crackled with the replacement of the handset and the gates clicked and whirred before slowly swinging open to welcome Knight and Culverhouse in like old friends.

'Why does he have these gates and walls?' Knight asked, 'He's not got a much bigger place than any of his neighbours and they've all got open driveways.'

'His neighbours probably aren't gangsters and crack dealers.'

'You'd be surprised. Some of the things that go on behind the most innocent of doors would amaze you.'

'Nothing amazes me any more, Knight,' Culverhouse said.

He brought the car to a stop just outside the red brick porch, its twin arches framing the impressive red door. Before they had even reached the door, it opened to reveal the man who Wendy assumed must be Gary McCann. She reckoned he must be just over six feet tall, his greying-white quiff adding at least an extra two inches to his height. He had the eyes and jowls of a hardened criminal, she had to admit, but he certainly cut a respectable figure in his open-necked suit and highly-polished patent leather Oxfords.

'Nice little place you've got here, Gary. What line of work are you in at the moment?' Culverhouse asked.

'Investments, mostly. In local businesses.' Gary McCann smiled.

'So I hear.'

'You not made Superintendent yet then, Inspector?' he said, ushering the pair through into his large living room. The huge open fire dominated the far wall, with three green leather sofas arranged around it.

'I think that's about as bloody likely as you being hailed as the next Mother Teresa, don't you?'

'Oh, I don't know. I do an awful lot for the local community. I'm very well known around these parts.'

'Yes, but Mother Teresa mostly did good,' Culverhouse said.

'I've done no bad, you know that, Inspector. You must have seen my record, what there is of it. Not a single conviction for a single crime. Even Nelson Mandela had a criminal conviction.'

'Mandela now, are you?' Culverhouse said. 'And yes, I'm very familiar with your police record as it happens. An awful lot of arrests on suspicion.'

'But nothing ever proven, isn't that right?'

'That doesn't make you the Good Samaritan, Gary. It just means we've not managed to catch you yet.'

'Yet?'

'Oh, yes. You know I'm going nowhere until I've got your bollocks stapled to my last arrest sheet.'

Gary McCann laughed. 'I like you, Jack. You've got balls.'

'So have you. For now.'

Gary McCann shoved his hands in his trouser pockets and smiled. 'Anyone fancy some coffee? I've got some Ethiopian stuff in.'

'Yes please,' Culverhouse replied. 'Extra strychnine for me.'

'I was going to give you a double dose anyway, Inspector. And what about your colleague here? Sorry, I don't know your name. These senior officers can be terrible rude when it comes to introductions.'

'Wendy. DS Wendy Knight.'

'Wendy. That's a lovely name.'

'That's DS Knight to you, McCann,' Culverhouse interjected.

'Oh, I thought we were all on first name terms, Jack?'

'We are, but she hasn't had her gloved finger up your arsehole as many times as I have.'

McCann smiled again and let out a small chuckle as he headed into the kitchen.

'Nice place,' Wendy said to Culverhouse as she heard the clanging of mugs and cutlery.

'Amazing what the proceeds of crime can buy.'

'He can't have done anything too bad, guv. If he's the

gangland mobster you make him out to be we'd have been able to nail something on him by now.'

'You ever tried nailing jelly to a wall?'

'Can't say I have,' Wendy replied.

'Try it. The day you get that to stick is the day we get this to stick.'

'Sorry, only got instant, I'm afraid,' Gary McCann said as he handed over the mugs to Knight and Culverhouse. 'Must've run out of the other stuff.'

'Make a habit out of sneaking up on people, do you Gary?' Culverhouse asked.

'I don't know what you mean, Inspector. Would you like sugar?'

'I'm sweet enough.'

'Indeed. And perhaps that coffee isn't the most bitter thing in this room either, eh?' McCann said, smiling.

'I'm not bitter, McCann. Every time you slip through my fingers it only makes me more fucking determined to nail you the next time.'

'Well, something has to get you up in the morning, I suppose. Now that your wife isn't here to do it.'

Culverhouse began to grind his teeth, his eyes widening at McCann's remark.

'Oh, sorry. Are we getting a bit too personal? Or was I not meant to know that?'

'It's hardly top secret information,' Culverhouse said, almost whispered, through gritted teeth.

'Nothing ever is, Inspector. Nothing ever is. Not in a small town like this. So, how can I help you? I presume you're not here for the Daz Doorstep Challenge.'

'We wanted to speak to you about someone we believe you might have known. A Bob Arthurs.'

'Bob? Radley Stationery Bob? Yeah, I know him. Why?'

'Well he's a very stationary Bob at the moment. He's dead.'

'Dead?' McCann replied. 'Oh dear, that is a shame. What happened?'

'I was rather hoping you could tell me. How did you know Bob Arthurs?'

'Well, he was one of my clients, a business partner. I had invested in his company.'

'In what sense?'

'He sold me some of his shares. Temporarily, like. They were short on readies so I bought out some of Bob's stake in the company. He was going to be buying them back over the course of a few years, only he'd fallen into a bit of trouble recently.'

'Trouble?' Wendy asked, trying to make her mark on the conversation.

'Yeah. Couldn't pay back the money a couple of times.'

'That's remarkably open of you, McCann,' Culverhouse said. 'You going to tell us what happened?'

'That is what happened, Inspector. The last I saw of Bob was over a month ago when I popped in to see how business was.'

'And how was it?'

'Not great, but everyone's having a tough time of it, aren't they?'

'I don't think many are having a tougher time than Bob Arthurs at the moment, if you ask me,' Culverhouse replied.

'Well, no. We've all got our health, I suppose. That's the only thing that old Bob had, really, truth be told.'

'And now he's had that taken from him as well. Who'd do a thing like that, Gary?'

'I've no idea. You mean he was murdered?'

'I mean he was brutally fucking slaughtered.'

Gary McCann began to pace in front of the fire-place, rubbing his chin with his hand, his head slightly aslant as he seemed to be digesting the news. Wendy glanced at Culverhouse, noting his unimpressed look.

'Save it for the interview room, McCann. We'll be needing copies of your accounts regarding your business with Bob Arthurs and Radley Stationery. I presume you do have accounts?'

'Of course I do. I'm very good at keeping records, as you know, Inspector. You'll have to get them sent over by my accountant, though. Here's his card. Is there anything else I can do for you?'

'I'm sure we'll be in contact in due course.'

Gary McCann stood, almost theatrically, one hand in his trouser pocket, the other waving to Knight and Culverhouse as they drove back down the gravel drive towards the now-open gates.

'Fucking smarmy bastard. I can't fucking wait to nail him over this,' Culverhouse said, his white knuckles gripping the steering wheel.

'You reckon the accounts will have holes in, then?'

'Like a sieve, Knight. Like a fucking sieve.'

19

The steel wheels clattered on the rails as the Class 319 roared into the station, bringing with it a warm gust of wind. The air whoomphed as each set of double doors passed the spot on which Helen was stood.

Eventually, the train came to a halt and the doors made a series of rapid bleeping noises before they opened. She stepped aside to let the alighting passengers off before stepping onto the train herself. It was always handy when more people got off than on, as it meant she'd be able to get a seat for the journey. Not that sitting on a sticky twenty-year-old seat next to an empty sandwich wrapper and a well-thumbed copy of the *Metro* was much to look forward to.

She glanced into the first-class compartment a little further down the carriage. A glass screen and a little bit of tissue paper for a headrest cover. Hardly the height of luxury, she thought, yet the train company were charging people double the price to sit in there.

She had tried telling herself that she wouldn't make an effort; he would just have to make do with how she came. It had never bothered him before, after all. Not that he'd ever taken much notice. Here she was, though, her glowing blonde hair straightened and flicked out at the ends, delicately glancing off her shoulders. She felt anything but delicate. She knew time had been kind to her in some ways and evil in others.

She'd had the internal battle over whether to just turn up as she was in order to show him that she didn't care for his opinion and was now a free woman, or whether she should go the whole hog and get herself properly tarted up to make him jealous of what he'd done and lost. In the end, she'd opted for a bit of both. Sitting on the fence, as always.

She cursed Em for not coming with her. She didn't want to meet him, she said. After all that Helen had told her about him, she said, she quite hoped she would never even get the opportunity to bump into him. She certainly wasn't going to try and see him voluntarily. Helen had chided Em for leaving her to do this on her own. She must have known it wasn't going to be easy for her, but it had to be done. Inside, she hated him too, but still. It had to be done. Things had to be said and the air had to be cleared. After all, surely it was all water under the bridge now?

It hadn't been hard to find him, especially as he had never actually gone anywhere. She knew he wouldn't have. She knew what a territorial creature he was — certainly not one to embrace change in any sense of the word.

She had no clue as to how she was going to explain to him why she'd done it. Of course, she knew why she'd done it but it made it no easier to explain things to him. The more that time had passed, the harder it had got. At first it was easy to say nothing and cut loose. The freedom had been new and liberating. As the dust had settled she had begun to realise that he deserved an explanation. The more the dust settled, though, the harder it became to walk across the floor for fear of leaving footprints.

She knew he'd feel betrayed and hurt, even now. He always had been one to hold a grudge and she doubted very much whether he would have changed. They say everyone deserves a second chance, but what about a third or a fourth? No. She knew it. He would never change.

20

The living room at 9 Vicarage Road was eerily silent despite the presence of Sylvia Arthurs, Jack Culverhouse and Wendy Knight. Sylvia sat in an armchair, holding a framed picture of her husband which she caressed with her thumb as she smiled through salty tears.

Wendy was the first to break the uncomfortable silence. 'I know this must be hard for you, Mrs Arthurs, but we need to ask some questions about your husband's death. Any information we have will help us find out exactly what happened to Bob.'

'I don't know what I can tell you, officer. I really don't,' the woman said. Wendy noted that she seemed to be holding good memories of her husband. That was something, at least.

'We need to know if your husband knew a man called Gary McCann. We believe they may have been in business together in some form.' Wendy could see from Sylvia's reaction that she did, indeed, know of Gary McCann. The flickering of the eyes and the short, sharp, hardly-noticeable intake of breath told her all she needed to know. 'Only we've received some information stating that Gary McCann may have invested in some of your husband's shares in Radley Stationery. Did you know anything about this?'

Sylvia Arthurs thought for a moment. She knew it was no use trying to lie. They probably knew everything anyway. 'Yes. Yes, I did.'

'And what was your opinion on it?' Culverhouse asked.

'Well, I was perfectly happy with it. Bob didn't have the money to keep his side of the business going and Gary stepped up and helped him out.'

'Financially?'

'Yes, that too. He helped Bob get the business back on track. Without him, the company would have folded long ago. It's thanks to him that I'm even sat in this house, if I'm honest.'

'With all due respect, from what we've seen, Mrs Arthurs, it doesn't look as though Radley Stationery was anywhere near back on track,' Wendy said. 'The business was haemorrhaging money and your husband must have been, too.'

'Are you saying... Do you think Bob might have committed suicide?' Sylvia asked.

'Not unless he managed to cave his own face in with a baseball bat and then jump in an acid bath before tying himself to a chair in his own warehouse, no,' Culverhouse said.

Wendy's eyes shot over to him. The man's tact astounded her.

'We think he may have been murdered as part of a grudge,' he added.

Sylvia Arthurs spoke, though visibly shocked. 'No, not Gary McCann. He wouldn't do that. He has been good to us. He's a good man, and he's been good to me since Bob died.'

'What do you mean he's been good to you since Bob died, Mrs Arthurs?'

'Well, I know it hasn't been long, but he's been really supportive since I heard the news. I mean, I know obviously everyone has been supportive, but it's mostly just words, isn't it? Not Gary, though. He gave me... a gift.' With this, Sylvia Arthurs stood up from her armchair and crossed the room to the sideboard. She opened the middle cupboard door and drew out two large jiffy bags. 'These were in my porch when I got home yesterday.'

Culverhouse opened the bag, looking at Sylvia for any clue as to what might be inside. Drawing his hand out, he brought with it a large bundle of used twenty-pound notes. Both jiffy bags were stuffed full.

'Ten thousand pounds, Inspector. Look at the note,' Sylvia said.

Inside the second jiffy bag, Culverhouse spotted the folded sheet of white A4 paper, which he duly unfolded and read. There, in the neatly typed and printed font were the words:

Your husband was a good man. Take this as a gift.
G McC.

He read the note twice more. 'Why would Gary McCann give you ten thousand pounds in cash, Mrs Arthurs?'

'I have no idea. I told you he was a kind man.'

'We'll have to take this in as evidence, I'm sure you'll understand.'

'Oh, yes. Of course. I've no idea what I'll do with all that money, anyway. Not now that I'm...' Sylvia's voice trailed off as her mouth refused to form the word.

. . .

Once outside, Knight and Culverhouse got into the unmarked Volvo and sat silently for a few moments, both knowing what the other wanted to say. It was always going to be Culverhouse who had the first word.

'I told you. I fucking told you Gary McCann was a lying bastard. All that bloody bollocks about being so surprised that Bob Arthurs had snuffed it, and all the time he's been sending fucking presents to his wife. But it still doesn't make any sense. Why would he do it?'

'Maybe he wanted to show Sylvia that he wasn't such a bad man after all,' Wendy said. 'Perhaps he felt that Bob Arthurs needed to go, but he felt no malice towards Sylvia. Nothing personal, that kind of thing. He must have known that Sylvia would be saddled with Bob's debts after he'd gone. Even criminals have a nice side.'

'Not this one, he doesn't. Gary McCann has never cared for a little old lady before. Hell, in his younger days he was known for mugging them. And anyway, if he wanted to make sure Sylvia wouldn't be left with the debt, why would he not just write it off in the first place and let Bob live? Wipe the ten grand off the company's debts instead. Same amount of money, and no dead body on your hands.'

'Or your conscience,' Wendy added.

Culverhouse snorted. 'Gary McCann wouldn't know the meaning of the word. No, something's definitely not right. We need to do some digging, Knight. There's something fishy going on with McCann and I'm going to find out what.'

21

Secretly, Jack Culverhouse had always liked doing press conferences. Although they were a pain in the arse, they usually threw up some good leads. Of course, there were the usual cranks and time-wasters, but overall it was a good exercise and it showed the public that the police were doing something.

Generally speaking, opening parts of enquiries up to the public didn't tend to be all that useful. In fact, the number of crank calls and false leads could often hamper an investigation, which was why press conferences were ever only organised when there was a significant public interest in the case or, as in this instance, when the police were completely and utterly stuck. Of course, that wasn't the line which tended to be fed to the Great British public.

The Mildenheath Police insignia was emblazoned on the wall behind Culverhouse as he gingerly stepped towards his seat and sat down. Taking a cursory sip of water from the glass in front of him, he shuffled his papers and tapped the microphone in front of him before beginning to speak. He knew what he was doing — he'd done it many times before — but looking concerned yet assured was a requisite skill as far as police public relations were concerned. Culverhouse was certainly not one to care for PR, but having fewer pissed off members of the public certainly made his life a lot easier.

'Ladies and gentlemen, I am Detective Chief Inspector Jack Culverhouse of Mildenheath CID. To my left is Chief Constable Charles Hawes, and to my right is Detective Sergeant Luke Baxter. I am here today to launch an appeal for information on the death of one Robert Arthurs, known as Bob, of Vicarage Road, Mildenheath. Mr Arthurs was a businessman, a partner in a local stationery firm. Mr Arthurs' body was found early on Wednesday morning by his business partner at the warehouse unit where they worked. We have reason to believe that Mr Arthurs' death was suspicious and are appealing for any information that may help catch his killer. Any questions?'

As Wendy sat in the incident room watching the

action unfold on the news channel, she grinned at Culverhouse's short and succinct address. That smirking git Baxter was doing him no favours, though.

A hand rose from the crowd and a voice spoke. 'DCI Culverhouse, Adam Reynolds, Mildenheath Gazette. You mentioned that Bob Arthurs' business partner, Donald Radley, found his body on Wednesday morning. Is Mr Radley a suspect in the investigation?'

'No. We are satisfied that Donald Radley had no motive for killing Bob Arthurs and that we have established his whereabouts during the time that Mr Arthurs is believed to have died. That is not an avenue we are pursuing.'

'Sam Rigby, Blaze Radio. You mentioned that you have reason to believe that Bob Arthurs' death was suspicious. What are the circumstances that lead you to believe this?'

Culverhouse sighed. This was a dilemma which had been discussed in full in the incident room prior to the press conference. It was usual practice to withhold some details of serious crime cases in order to be able to weed out crank callers later in the investigation. Due to the distinct lack of evidence in the Bob Arthurs murder case, it had been decided that the grisly details would be withheld only unless specifically asked for. Even then, they'd have to be carefully managed. It wasn't easy to only leak a couple of details when you didn't have many in the first place. It hadn't taken Sam Rigby long to blow that plan out of the water.

'Bob Arthurs' body had been badly beaten. We believe he had been initially attacked with a baseball bat. His body was then subjected to a hydrochloric acid attack.'

'At what point during the attack did Mr Arthurs die, Inspector?' Adam Reynolds from the Mildenheath Gazette had poked his head above the parapet once again. Culverhouse knew from past experience that Reynolds was like a dog with a bone once he got going.

'We're not totally sure at the moment. The pathologist also saw evidence of strangulation but there were no signs of a struggle. This may have been due to Mr Arthurs being unconscious at the time due to the earlier head trauma.'

'What information are you looking for at this time?' Adam Reynolds asked, beginning to dominate the press conference.

'We're looking for anyone who may have known Bob Arthurs and can provide us with some more insight into his life. He seems to have been a very secretive man, but someone clearly had a grudge against him. We would also like people locally to be vigilant and let us know if they spot any odd behaviour in close friends or relatives which may be linked to the events of Tuesday night and Wednesday morning. Please do call the incident room if you think you may have some information, no matter how insignificant. Even the smallest details can help enormously.'

22

The incident room was abuzz with ringing phones and the chatter of numerous officers frantically taking notes from all manner of callers. Culverhouse had noticed that public appeals tended to have two effects.

One was that the local loners and attention seekers would phone up with made up or imagined information and theories. The other was that those who had information which would actually be of some use were convinced that the case was so big and advanced that their information on that suspicious-looking car or the odd behaviour of their spouse was not worth mentioning.

Culverhouse sauntered about the room, glancing at the notepads and computer screens over the shoulders of the officers. The investigation was still fairly new, but it seemed to Wendy that Culverhouse had visibly aged; his once-crisp white shirt now hanging loosely over the top of his trousers, stray locks of hair teasing his glistening forehead.

'Anything of note yet, Baxter?' Culverhouse asked, speaking to the young Detective Sergeant.

'Nothing, sir. Although I did speak to one little old lady who was convinced she actually saw Danielle Levy disappear on Friday lunchtime.'

'What? Really?' Culverhouse asked.

'Yep. Sucked up by a beam of light into a waiting spacecraft, by all accounts. She even reckons the aliens left her a message not to tell anyone, but she decided to defy them anyway. Considered it her public duty to the human race in—' Baxter consulted his notepad. '"Our struggle against our reptilian overlords".'

'I wish she bloody hadn't,' Culverhouse replied. 'Have we had anything that's actually been of any use?'

'Not from what I'm seeing, sir. Just theories and crackpots.'

'Right. Steve, anything on the Bob Arthurs case?' he said, addressing DS Wing, who was cradling a mug of black coffee.

'Nothing, guv. We seem to be at a dead end on that one. Oh, except we did have four calls asking us if Radley Stationery would still be open for business today.

Seems there's a demand for branded pencil cases at the moment.'

'Can't beat a bit of sympathy and patience, eh? Any callers mentioned Gary McCann at all? Be interesting to see if his name crops up in connection with anything.'

'I don't think so, guv. Not that I've heard, anyway. But the way Bob Arthurs died, his business connections with McCann and the ten grand he gave his missus — that's got to go some way towards things. Do we have enough information for a search warrant, do you reckon?'

Culverhouse removed a sheet of folded paper from his back pocket. 'Apparently so. Looks like I caught the Magistrate in a good mood this morning. In fact,' Culverhouse said, glancing at his watch, 'the forensics boys should be on their way down there now. I think I'll pop in and see how Mr McCann's getting on. I quite fancy a bit of afternoon entertainment.'

'He'll be only too pleased to see you, guv,' DS Wing replied, smiling.

23

The gates to Gary McCann's house were already open as Culverhouse negotiated the gravel driveway and parked his car in front of the house. McCann was standing in the driveway, watching closely as white-suited forensics officers entered and exited the house with all manner of technical equipment and personal belongings.

Culverhouse gave him a huge, beaming grin as he got out of his car and walked across the crunching gravel towards him.

'I hope your men know what they're doing, Inspector. I'd like to see what grounds you've got for searching my bloody house.'

'Well, the other option is to arrest you and then we

can search the place under Section 18 without needing a warrant. Would that be more to your satisfaction?' Culverhouse replied, smirking.

'Arrest me for what, exactly? You've got no evidence of anything, which is why you've had to go down this route to find some. What did you tell the Magistrate? That I'd not comply? That there would be some sort of written confession hidden somewhere in my house?'

'No need to get agitated, Mr McCann. If you're innocent then I'm sure all will be fine.'

'*When* I'm innocent, it'll be even less fine, Inspector Culverhouse, because I'll be having a little conversation with your Chief Constable about this.'

Culverhouse knew that Hawes would be more than happy to speak to Gary McCann about a few choice cases he'd looked at in the past. In fact, he was pretty sure that the Chief Constable would be very keen to re-open a few dry cases and tie up some loose ends where the CPS had previously decided a case couldn't be tried. He was quite sure, though, that the conversation between Hawes and McCann would be somewhat one-directional.

'I'm sure he'd be delighted to speak with you, Mr McCann. He's probably got quite a few questions of his own and would be more than happy to delve a little more deeply into your whiter-than-white dealings. Now, do you have any questions regarding this particular investigation?'

'Just the one. What the bloody hell do you think you're playing at?'

'We're investigating the murder of Bob Arthurs, Mr McCann. Did our officers not explain that to you?' Culverhouse asked innocently and facetiously.

'What, and you think I killed the silly old bugger?'

'Oh, I don't believe anyone's said that, Mr McCann. But there are a few things we need to check out. I think you might have information that could help advance our investigation. Perhaps a few things that you aren't telling us.'

'Very tactful, DI Culverhouse. Not like you at all. Starting to go a bit soft in your old age, are you? Or are you just starting to get over the fact that your missus did a runner?'

Culverhouse visibly stiffened at the mention of his wife — a sign which didn't go unnoticed by Gary McCann, who responded with a knowing smirk.

'People die all the time, Inspector. You know that. Sometimes it's an accident, sometimes it's more deliberate. And people go missing quite a lot, too. Who knows why? Sometimes they go of their own volition, and sometimes they don't. Sometimes no-one knows where they are, and sometimes someone does. It's a mysterious old world, isn't it, Inspector?'

'I presume we're still talking about Bob Arthurs,' Culverhouse said, knowing damned well exactly what Gary McCann was talking about.

McCann just smiled. 'You tell me, Inspector. You tell me.'

As Culverhouse walked into the house and entered the dining room, he watched as the forensics team sifted through reams of paperwork from the sideboard cabinet and bagged the occasional item of interest.

He heard Gary McCann's footsteps on the parquet flooring behind him.

'Don't make too much of a mess, will you, boys? I've only just had this bloody carpet put in.'

'I'm sure my men will do whatever it takes, Mr McCann. Anyway, I'm quite sure you've got nothing to worry about. You've already said you had nothing to do with anything, so this is all academic, isn't it?'

'If you were that sure, Inspector, you wouldn't be here ripping my bloody house apart. You'd be out looking for the real killer or someone who can actually be of some use to you.'

'Oh, I only said I was *quite* sure, Mr McCann.'

Gary McCann swaggered slightly as he took a step towards Culverhouse, their noses barely inches apart. 'Let's cut the bullshit, shall we, Inspector? So you reckon I bumped off Bob Arthurs, do you?'

24

Jack Culverhouse, man of logic, was sometimes entirely illogical. He had long wondered why he bothered to walk to the local shop and buy that day's copy of *The Times* at nine o'clock in the evening, almost a full twenty-four hours after the news was barely fresh in the first place. The *BBC News* website and a copy of *Crossword Monthly* would be an adequate replacement, but nothing could beat the creature comfort of a fresh newspaper in the evening.

He could feel the sweat and oils from his hands ruining the print on the front page as he unintentionally defaced the image of a smiling Michelle Obama. As he walked up the hill from the parade of shops and back onto the main road, Jack's heart skipped a beat.

The figure standing at the bus stop looked a little too

familiar. A familiar stranger. On any other day, he would have walked past without even taking a second glance. But today, he knew, it must have been his brain playing tricks on him. It happened at this time every year, around the time of the anniversary. Calendars might be inert piles of paper, but they had an uncanny way of bringing back bad memories with alarming regularity. He told himself that she had been occupying his mind far too much recently; he was even starting to see her in the street.

It was impossible, though. The brain was a clever thing. He knew that. Perhaps this was how he wanted to imagine her: gaunt, drawn and a relic of her former self. Maybe he wished all these things on her as a punishment for walking out on him and taking their only child with her. She had no reason to be in Mildenheath. The last thing he heard was that she had briefly visited her parents in Cornwall before heading for the Southampton ferry barely days after having left him. He knew through his contacts that she hadn't re-entered the country.

His mind was playing tricks on him, he decided, and picked up his pace as he walked on.

* * *

Shit. Had he seen her? She fucking hoped not. *Stupid, stupid idea.* She wanted desperately to speak to him, to have it out with him, but how was she ever going to do that if she couldn't even make eye contact with him without diving behind a bloody bus shelter?

The whole thing had been one stupid idea. She didn't need to come back, so why had she? She'd trekked halfway across Europe without even knowing what she was going to do when she got there. She'd played out the scene a hundred times in her mind, but every time it happened differently. For her, it was just a case of putting the whole episode to bed. Once and for all.

She drew forcefully on her cigarette, the calming nicotine filling her lungs, her hands shaking and flicking ash over her jacket as she tried to hug herself warm. Mildenheath was always cold at night, no matter what time of the year it was. She'd not experienced cold evenings since she'd left. Something else she hadn't missed.

A passing police car slowed before pulling into the bus stop. Great. Fucking great.

'You all right, love?' the officer in the passenger seat asked, having wound down his window.

'Fine, thanks.'

'You sure?'

'Yes. Fine, thanks.'

'Only buses don't run from here at this time of night.'

She cocked her head to the side and looked at the sodden timetable which adorned the bus shelter. Shit. The last bus was at 19:28. Half-past seven, not half-past nine.

'Oh, right. Sorry. I misread the timetable. I thought there was another one at half past.'

'You not from round here?'

'Not any more, no,' she replied.

The officer opened his door and got out of the car. 'Mind if we take some details from you, love?'

'Why? Misreading a bus timetable isn't an offence,' she said, stubbing out her cigarette under her shoe.

'No, but we've had a lot of reports of... well, street-walkers around this area recently. We just need to take a few details. If everything matches up then it won't be a problem.'

Street-walkers? This is what her life had come to: quivering in a bus stop with only a Marlboro Light for company, being mistaken for a prostitute. She knew one thing for sure: she couldn't give them her real name. She couldn't even give them her false name. Who knew how sophisticated the police computers were in the UK these days? It had been easy enough when she left, but things would be different now.

'Listen, I'm not a hooker, all right? I misread the timetable.'

'Where are you staying tonight?' the other officer asked, having got out of the car and walked round to the pavement, his thumbs lodged in the sides of his vest.

'With an old friend. I'm not back for long. Just catching up.'

'They live local, your friend?'

'Fairly local, yeah. Look, it's fine. I'll just have to walk there.'

'Right, OK. Well be careful, all right? Lots of nasty sorts around here at this time of night,' the first officer said, before beckoning his colleague back over towards the car.

She knew exactly what nasty sorts were around. Oh, she knew.

25

DCI Culverhouse sat in his living room armchair and glanced forlornly at the photographs of Danielle Levy. Barely seventeen years old and, in his heart of hearts, he knew the increasing likelihood was that she would be found dead. Once forty-eight hours had passed, the odds were approaching certainty. That left two questions: who and why?

The why was probably more difficult than the who. A chance abduction seemed unlikely, particularly as she'd lived in a fairly busy part of the town. People just didn't tend to be successfully abducted in a busy town in the middle of the day without anyone noticing. Small children, perhaps, but not streetwise seventeen-year-olds.

He found himself lost in a world of imagination as

Danielle almost came to life before his eyes. Even though it was rare that he ever met any of the victims while they were alive, every time he investigated a murder or potential murder case he almost brought the person to live in his own mind. Having to research every aspect of their past, their family and their life meant that the victim became real once again. Sometimes, it helped. Other times, it made things very tough indeed.

He had visions of Danielle getting ready for a night out, sitting around with her friends, discussing boys and make-up. She would have had no problem getting into nightclubs, that was for sure. Her looks were mature, and she would certainly pass for being in her twenties, no problem at all.

All girls grow up too quickly nowadays. Jack's own daughter would be almost in her teens by now. Not far off Danielle's age. To him, she had almost become ageless now. She'd been so young the last time he saw her, he couldn't envisage her being anything other than the smiling child that he'd known and lost, grinning and laughing as her pigtails swished around at the back of her head.

The pain and sorrow choked him up as his visions of Danielle Levy became visions of his own daughter, her features transforming before his very eyes. It was true to say that he had no idea what she would look like nowadays, but he was sure she'd be beautiful. He could see her all grown up. The boys and make-up, the getting into nightclubs. The screams of terror. The dark, congealing blood and empty, staring eyes.

Shaking the vision from his mind's eye, he reminded himself that Danielle Levy could still be alive, his daughter even more so. He was not a religious man, but he hoped to God he would see them both soon.

Culverhouse was jolted out of his phantasmal daydream by the ringing of his mobile phone. As he pressed to answer the call, he could utter nothing more committal than an absent-minded 'Mmmm?'

'Guv, it's Frank Vine. Listen, we've received a call from a dog walker. They've found a body. We think it might be Danielle Levy.'

26

The dense wooded area sat aside the train line between Upper Berrydale and Middlebrook, a peaceful and tranquil location but for the cutting sound of London-bound trains every few minutes. It was clear to Culverhouse that sunlight rarely permeated any part of this wood. It smelt dark and musty, hundreds of years' worth of rotting leaves and vegetation compacting to form the rich compost on which he now stood.

'Right, where is it?'

'Down there, guv,' Frank Vine offered, pointing to the crater-sized dip in the forest floor which was coated with a thick layer of deep-green ivy. Scenes of Crime officers swarmed around the wood, looking for any small clues which could be of use.

Grunting to himself, Culverhouse scuttled down

into the crab position and worked his heels down the steep edge of the ravine. Losing his footing just once or twice, he righted himself at the bottom of the dip and almost overcompensated but for the saving grace of a well-placed tree trunk.

'Just to your right, guv. Over towards the birch tree. You'll see the newspapers.' Makes a change from black bin liners, Culverhouse supposed.

He made his way, slowly but surely, towards the body, being careful not to tread anywhere he shouldn't.

'What the fuck is this?' Culverhouse barked.

'Is there a problem, guv?' Frank replied.

'Yes, there's a fucking problem. You told me you had a body.'

'It is a body, guv. No doubting that. SOCO confirmed it.'

'It's not a fucking body, DS Vine. Bodies have heads, arms, legs and a torso. This is a half-formed cadaver with the majority of the skin and bone melted into mush.'

'Well yeah, but "body" was easier to say on the phone, guv.'

Culverhouse could see that what was left of the body parts had been wrapped in newspaper as an afterthought, seeing as most of it was in more-or-less pristine condition. More than could be said for what was left of the body. He was no expert, but even he could see that it had been subjected to an acid attack *in situ*, and had not simply been dumped afterwards. The cloying silt which surrounded her body had turned to glue, the process of biodegradation sped up by the chemical interference. The newspapers which covered the cadaver, though, were remarkably unscathed.

'Great. Fucking great. Has Dr Grey been down here yet?' Culverhouse asked.

'Yep, she's been and gone. She says she can't tell much from what's left and it'll be virtually impossible to tell the age and sex of the body, but she said she's 80% sure it's a woman between eighteen and forty years of age.'

'Nice and precise, then,' Culverhouse remarked sarcastically. 'Narrows it down to a few million people.'

'There is some good news, though, guv. Danielle Levy's handbag was found just a few feet away and Dr Grey reckons the general height and build fits the description we have of Danielle. She didn't want to commit, obviously, but I reckon she's pretty certain it's her.'

'Great. Just what we need,' Culverhouse said, rubbing his chin.

'Oh, and she said that the body definitely couldn't have been covered up before Saturday.'

'What? How can she be so sure?'

'Well, for a start, the newspaper's got Saturday's date on it.'

'What, so she was killed before and then covered up a couple of days later? Or she was kept alive somewhere and then killed?'

'That's what we're going to have to find out,' Frank replied.

27

The warm glow of the sun belied the dark cloud of grief which was soon to wash over 101 Heathcote Road. It was a job that every police officer hated. The only thing worse than seeing a dead, decaying, rotting body was having to tell their nearest and dearest what had happened to them. No matter how many times you had to do it throughout your career, it got no easier. To have to start with a lie; the pleasantries, the how-are-yous, the all-impending knowledge of what was to come, what was inevitable, eating away at every part of you.

It was why so many officers chose to get straight down to business. Many of them got straight to the point and told them why they were there as soon as the door was open. Others tended to beat around the bush and get through four or five cups of tea and twice as many fingernails before finally breaking the bad news.

Perhaps it was fortunate that Darren Parker had picked up on a facial expression, an atmosphere, when he opened the door that afternoon. The initial smile was eradicated by his sinking features. Wendy could swear that she had seen him age by ten years right in front of her.

'Mr Parker, we've come to speak to you and your wife about Danielle. Can we come in?'

'She's ... she's dead, isn't she?'

'Can we come in, Mr Parker?' Wendy replied. 'I'd much rather we spoke inside.'

Miriam Levy was sat, perched on the edge of an armchair, a scrunch of tissues clenched to her chin as she rocked her elbows on her knees. Her eyes told of pain and sorrow, but her voice said nothing.

'I'll get straight to the point,' DCI Culverhouse started, surprising no-one. 'We've found a... well, a body, of sorts, in the woods between Upper Berrydale and Middlebrook. We have reason to believe it might be Danielle.'

The last glowing embers of hope died visibly on the

faces of Darren Parker and Miriam Levy, the main fire already all but extinguished.

'Will we... will we need to identify her?' Danielle's step-father asked.

'That probably isn't a good idea, Mr Parker. We'd like to carry out a DNA match instead. We don't have Danielle's DNA on file, so we'll need to take an item of unwashed clothing. Either that or a hairbrush used exclusively by her. Might you have anything?'

'Well, yes, both. Do we need to get it now?' Miriam replied.

'In your own time. We understand how distressing this must be,' Wendy replied.

Darren Parker instead kept his eyes firmly fixed on Culverhouse.

'I'm no fool, Inspector. I know how these things work. The reason we can't identify her is because she's unidentifiable, isn't it?' Culverhouse said nothing, but diverted his eyes towards the cream carpet. 'So what makes you think it might be her in the first place? I mean, if you can't identify her...'

Wendy spoke on behalf of them both. 'Some of her belongings were found close by, Mr Parker. That doesn't immediately mean the body is Danielle's, but the location of both the body and her belongings is eight-and-a-half miles away from where she was last seen, so it does make it a lot more likely that there's a match.'

'Right. I see. Well, I'd better go and get some bits for you, then.'

It occurred to Wendy that Darren Parker was one of many different types of grievers. He was the rock. The one who tried to appear as the calm organiser, the steady force, but in private would break down worse than anyone else. Miriam Levy, on the other hand, was quite the opposite, being visibly torn from the inside out in front of their very eyes.

A few minutes later, Darren Parker re-entered the living room with two large sandwich bags, one dwarfing the hairbrush within it, the other almost at bursting point with the woollen jumper which it held. He handed them to Wendy.

'I picked them both up with the bags. So there weren't any more fingerprints or mixed DNA or whatever on them, you know.'

'Thanks. That's very helpful.'

'So. When will we know? We can't just sit here not knowing whether she's dead or not.'

'It shouldn't be long, Mr Parker. I know every minute can feel like an hour, but we'll do our best to ensure your mind can be at rest as soon as possible.'

'Thank you. I just... I just don't know what I would do if it was Danielle.'

28

Mildenheath General Hospital was a place that Wendy would be glad if she never saw again. The cold white walls, the beeping of machinery, the deathly rattle of old people coughing. The reminders of Michael. She was only pleased that now she was here for happier reasons. In a way, the juxtaposition was beautiful. What had come out of absolute tragedy was wonderful, serene.

She had told herself that she had come to terms with her new state of being. Wendy the mother. Inside, she knew that she was no mother. She was a police officer and that was that. The everlasting memory of Robert, though, would change all of that. To be carrying his baby made her feel as though a part of him was still with her. A part of him which hadn't suffered, hadn't died in writhing agony at the hands of her brother, Michael. The truth be told, she had rarely been happier.

As she sat in the waiting room of the maternity ward, the fabric of the chair grew softer, enveloping her with warmth and comfort. This was the maternal glow, she thought. The miracle. Her over-rational head tried to tell her that it was purely hormonal, that this wasn't her, but she knew better than to listen to her head. Her heart was telling her otherwise. Her heart was beating for two.

* * *

'DCI Culverhouse? Liz Prior here from forensics. I've got some rather interesting news for you, as it happens.'

'Go on.'

'Well, first of all, the DNA found on the body in the woods matches that of Danielle Levy.'

'So it's her?'

'Yes, I'm afraid so. The thing is, there's a big cross-over match between another investigation I believe you're currently working on.'

Culverhouse's eyes lit up. 'Go on.'

'It's regarding the samples taken from Gary McCann's house. We found a number of hairs which we've identified as belonging to someone you may be interested in. Danielle. This puts her as having been in his house and car on at least one occasion fairly recently.'

'Fucking brilliant! Well done, Liz. I owe you one.' Culverhouse didn't replace the handset, but simply pressed the hook button before releasing it and dialling Wendy's mobile number.

'Knight. Culverhouse. I need you at the station as soon as you can. There's been a very interesting development.'

'I'm waiting to see the midwife for my appointment, guv. Is it urgent?'

'Put it this way — your baby's going nowhere at the moment. As for Gary McCann, that's another story.'

29

Gary McCann smiled smugly as he leaned back on the two rear legs of the chair in the interview room, his hands behind his head.

'Worried about something, McCann?' Culverhouse asked.

'Why would I have anything to worry about, Inspector?'

'In my experience, the cool, calm characters become just a little bit too cool and calm when they're as guilty as sin.'

'And in my experience, police officers start to make up all sorts of ludicrous psychological theories when they get desperate at having nothing else in their arsenal,' McCann replied, smirking at Culverhouse.

'Oh, my arsenal is positively overflowing, Mr

McCann. Tell me, do you know a girl called Danielle Levy?'

'Sorry, what has this got to do with Bob Arthurs?' McCann said, dismissively.

'I'm not sure myself. Not just yet, anyway. What I do know, though, is that Danielle Levy went missing from her house on Friday lunchtime and hasn't been seen since. I also know that in the process of scouring your house for material in connection with the murder of Bob Arthurs, we found a number of hairs belonging to Danielle. Can you explain how they got there?'

Gary McCann slowly lowered the front of his chair, allowing the legs to come to a rest on the floor with a clop as he brought his hands down in front of him, crossing them on the table. 'Absolutely not, Inspector. I've never heard of her.'

'I would like to remind you that this interview is being recorded, Mr McCann, and that we have evidence which shows that Danielle Levy has been in both your house and car recently. Do you want to reconsider your answer at all?'

'That's impossible,' McCann replied, clearly getting more agitated by the second. 'No-one else uses my car and we don't have other people around at the house. Not until we started holding your police parties for you in the past few days, anyway. If you've found anything, it's a fit-up. You've been trying to stitch things on me for years.'

'You'll have to come up with something better than that, McCann. The forensic evidence doesn't lie. Danielle Levy has been in your house and she has been in your car. And I want to know why.'

'I'm telling you. I ain't never heard of her, all right?'

'Have you had any parties at your house recently, Mr McCann?' Wendy said, trying to nudge the conversation in some sort of forward direction.

'No, I don't tend to go in for that. We're a very private household, know what I mean?'

'Hardly surprising,' Culverhouse added, drily.

'I mean, yeah, we have friends around occasionally but only the odd dinner party and that. And never with no-one called Danielle Levy, that's for sure.'

'And do you ever take anyone else in your car?' Wendy asked.

'Only my current wife, and she's tucked up safe and sound at home and definitely not lying dead anywhere.'

'Your first one is, though, isn't she?' Culverhouse replied.

'Listen, I can't speak for your forensics blokes, but I know damn well who's been in my house and I know damn well who hasn't. Now, unless I'm being fitted up, I'm afraid I can't help you, Inspector.'

30

Wendy crossed her arms as they stood outside the inter-view room.

'Fitted up? Who'd want to fit him up?'

'A lot of people, Knight. McCann's a vicious bastard and he doesn't care who he hurts. I'm damn sure he killed his first wife and everyone else knows it too. The worst thing is, he knows we know it and he also knows we can't do a fucking thing about it.'

Justice was cruel sometimes, and a lack of evidence meant a lack of a trial and a lack of conviction. In essence, the killer walked free. This, amongst other things, was what riled Jack Culverhouse the most about the modern police force.

'But surely if he's come that close to being caught before he's not likely to kill again on a whim. Besides, killing your wife is completely different to just popping off a business associate. It's not the sign of a serial killer. It just doesn't add up, guv.'

'A killer's a killer, Knight. And Gary McCann is a killer. I've been a copper long enough to know a killer when I see one.'

'But what reason would he have to kill Danielle Levy? He said himself he doesn't even know the girl.'

'That doesn't mean anything. McCann's good at lying through his teeth. For all we know, they could have been carrying on together and he did her in before she started gobbing off to her mates.'

'Pardon me, guv, but I can't see any reason why a seventeen-year-old girl would want to "carry on" with a greying, beer-bellied man with a criminal history.'

'You'd be surprised what attracts some women, Knight. Funnier things have happened.'

Wendy surreptitiously eyed Culverhouse before trying to work out whether she agreed or disagreed with his summary.

'Yeah, I think I probably would be surprised.'

'The fact of the matter is, Danielle Levy's hair was found in McCann's house and car. She was there. That's a fact. We just need to find out why.'

'And how do you suggest we do that when McCann swears blind he's never heard of her?'

'We go round and talk to the wife. I reckon she'd be a much easier pushover than he would. She's certainly far more likely to let something slip if we push hard enough, anyway.'

'We can't do that, guv. We don't have a warrant to enter again.'

'I don't need a warrant to ring the fucking doorbell,' Culverhouse replied angrily.

Back at Gary McCann's house, Knight and Culverhouse were pleased to see McCann's second and current wife, Imogen, tending to the front garden.

'See?' he said to Wendy. 'Didn't even need to ring the doorbell after all.'

Bringing the car to a halt on the sweeping gravel driveway, the pair got out and introduced themselves to Imogen McCann.

'Ah, Mrs McCann. I don't think we've met. Detective Chief Inspector Jack Culverhouse, Mildenheath Police. This is my colleague, Detective Sergeant Wendy Knight.'

'Yes, I've heard a lot about you,' the woman said, one eyebrow raised.

'I'm glad my reputation precedes me. Can we speak inside?'

. . .

Imogen McCann guided DCI Culverhouse and DS Knight into the spacious living room adorned with photographs and watercolour paintings. Culverhouse stood, one hand in his pocket, the other picking up photographs and examining them.

'Lots of photos you have here.'

'Yes.'

'None of your husband's ex-wife, I notice.'

'No. He doesn't like the reminders. Why would he? We've all moved on.'

'Oh. Rather odd,' Culverhouse said. 'I thought they got on quite well?'

'Well, yes, they did. He doesn't like the reminders of what happened to her, I mean. It's not exactly the sort of thing you want staring you in the face every day. Gary's been through hell with what happened to Tanya. Especially when you lot wouldn't leave him alone and tried to convict him of murdering her. It's outrageous the way you lot treat grieving families sometimes.'

'Believe me, Mrs McCann, if I had the time I'd try again. Unfortunately, we have other dead people to try and bring justice to. This time, I won't allow the system to let them down.'

'And what, you think Gary had something to do with Bob Arthurs' death too, I suppose?'

'Oh no, Mrs McCann. I've not even got onto the Bob Arthurs case yet. We're currently interviewing your husband in connection with the murder of Miss Danielle Levy,' Culverhouse read from his notepad, as if seeing the name for the first time.

'Who?'

'A seventeen-year-old girl from Heathcote Road. She went missing on Friday lunchtime and was found dead in the woods between Upper Berrydale and Middle-brook. We're not quite sure how she died, because her body had been so badly dissolved by industrial-strength hydrochloric acid. Do you need me to go on, Mrs McCann?'

Imogen McCann's face told Culverhouse all he needed to know in response to that question. 'But how could it have been Gary? That's ridiculous. Did he even know her?'

'That's what we're trying to find out. Do you know if your husband had been having any extra-marital affairs? One night stands? Playgirls?'

'Come off it, Inspector! Gary's a caring family man.'

Culverhouse almost exploded in a fit of laughter, leaving Wendy unsure as to whether it was real or purely for display purposes. 'Yeah, and I'm Diana fucking Ross. I just white-up for the day job.'

'Mrs McCann, did you ever suspect that your husband may have been unfaithful to you?' Wendy said, trying to inject some professionalism into the proceedings.

'No, never. I trust him and I know he wouldn't do that.'

'The thing is, we've found traces of Danielle Levy's hair in your house and in your husband's car.'

'Traces? What kind of traces?'

'Massive fucking clumps,' Culverhouse said bluntly.

'I don't see how that's possible. I mean... he...'

'I know this might be hard for you to digest, Mrs McCann' Wendy said, 'but I really need to you think hard as to whether your husband may have known Danielle Levy and how her hairs might have come to be in your house and car. Because, at the moment, it really isn't looking very good.'

Imogen McCann sat in silence for a few moments before speaking.

'Well. There is something.'

31

Once they'd got back to the incident room, the paper-work had continued to mount up. Fortunately for Wendy, Luke Baxter had been in a surprisingly good mood and had agreed to take care of some of it for her.

She had barely had time to sit down and take more than a sip of her coffee when the phone had rung.

Two minutes later, Wendy replaced the receiver, put the lid back on her pen and jogged towards Culver-house's office with the notepad in her hand.

'Guv? I've just had a call from a girl called Lyndsey Samuels. Says she was a school friend of Danielle Levy. She saw the appeal on TV and wanted to tell us about a boy she reckons Danielle had been seeing recently. Says it was nothing serious, but she thinks he was a bit of a troublemaker and might have something for us.'

'What's his name?'

'Shane Howard. Lives up Forkston Road.'

'Says it all, really. Perhaps we should go and have a chat.'

Forkston Road was known locally for harbouring a number of criminals. The houses were mostly council-owned or association housing, with a very high rate of unemployment. Shane Howard's family house was a simple two-up-two-down affair, nestled in the middle of four or five similar terraced properties. A light blue rusting Vauxhall Cavalier was parked jauntily on the road outside.

Culverhouse rang the doorbell and waited a few moments before the woman opened the door. Mutton dressed as lamb was the first thought that came into Culverhouse's mind. Not brilliant lamb, either. The enormous golden hooped earrings deflected the eye from the drooping cigarette and pockmarked skin of Shane Howard's mother.

'Yeah? Wot is it?'

'Mrs Howard? We've come to speak to your son, Shane.'

'Wot about? He ain't done nuffin' wrong. Why do you lot keep comin' round and givin' us 'assle?' Wendy was always amazed at how some people could spot a police officer a mile off, despite no-one having told them who they were. Guilty eyes see all, she thought.

'We're not trying to give anyone any hassle, Mrs Howard. We just want to speak to him as a possible witness in connection with a recent incident.'

'Well you won't find nuffin' 'ere. 'E's down the park, ain't he?'

'Which one?' Wendy asked.

'On Meadow Hill Lane. Probably wiv 'is mates. Don't go bovverin' 'im though, will ya?'

'We'll do what we need to do, thank you, Mrs Howard,' Culverhouse said as politely as he could.

They didn't stay a minute longer than they needed to.

Pulling the car in beside the tennis courts, Wendy was relieved to be in plain clothes and an unmarked car. She was pretty sure Shane Howard would spot them a mile off anyway, but they'd have a much better chance than they would rocking up in a glow-in-the-dark car with a bloody great light on the top.

Despite the tranquil surroundings, the park on Meadow Hill Lane was a notorious stomping ground for young thugs and layabouts. The old cricket pavilion made for the centre of much of the trouble, standing as it did aside the large open green area donned with football and cricket pitches and tennis courts.

'Plenty of them about, guv,' Wendy said, gesturing to the large group of teenagers sat around by the cricket pavilion. How will you know which one's him?'

'Oh, I'll know, don't you worry. Let's just say we've met once or twice before.'

'There's quite a few of them, though. What if things turn nasty? Think we should call for back-up?'

'Oh yeah, great idea, Knight. Get them to turn the sirens up extra loud as well. Maybe we can all have a big game of cricket afterwards.'

Making their way down the poorly-laid concrete path which ran down the side of the park, past the pavilion, Knight and Culverhouse approached the gang of youths.

'Oi oi! Anyone smell that?' one of them shouted.

'Yeah, smells like bacon!'

The group fell into a roar of rapturous laughter and mock applause.

'My old mate Inspector Culverhouse! Come to have a bit of a drink and a smoke with us, 'ave ya? Dirty ol' dog.'

'Shane Howard, we meet again.'

'I'll take that as a no, then. Only need to say, like. More for me, then.'

Shane Howard's gang of lemmings continued to laugh at his every comment, as if entranced by cult.

'We need to speak to you about Danielle Levy, Shane,' Culverhouse said calmly.

'Who?'

'Danielle Levy. We believe she may have been your girlfriend.'

'Hah, is that what you call it? Nah, we had a bit of a thing, like, but I wouldn't call her my girlfriend.' He took another drag on his cigarette.

'Fuck buddy, more like!' one of the group piped up, followed by more rapturous laughter.

'Whatever she was to you, we want to know what you might know about her murder,' Culverhouse said.

'Murder, eh? Can't say I can 'elp you, Inspector. If I 'ad to give you information on every girl I shagged, we'd be 'ere a long time, know what I mean? Don't even know 'alf their names, like.'

'Well, aren't you the big man? Make you feel big, does it? Using a girl for sex and not giving two shits when she ends up dead?'

'I never killed her, Inspector. Now piss off.'

'And how do I know that? You've had more criminal records than Cliff Richard.'

'Well, you'll 'ave to catch me to find out, won't ya?'

Roaring with laughter, Shane Howard stood up, dodged Culverhouse's outstretched arm and made off on his toes towards the gate on Meadow Hill Lane, his gang of yobs egging him on with every step.

'Go on, Shane! Leg it!' one yelled.

Culverhouse was quick to react, beginning only a couple of feet behind Shane Howard, yet unable to make any purchase on grabbing him. Wendy, slower to react, but quicker to gain, soon overtook the bumbling Culverhouse and began sprinting and gaining on Shane as her feet hammered into the concrete path, stumbling and stacking on the uneven surface as she went.

As Culverhouse gave up and slumped on the grass bank panting and wheezing, Wendy came within touching distance of Shane Howard as they approached the front gate of the park. As they reached the pavement on Meadow Hill Lane, Wendy managed to wrap her right arm around Shane's shoulder and yank him back towards her as they grappled for supremacy. Not caring much for guidelines and methods of restraint noted in Blackstone's, Wendy began kicking at the legs of Shane Howard in an attempt to knock him off balance and restrain him until DCI Culverhouse, now back on his feet and moving towards them like a slow mound of jelly, came back on the scene.

With a grunting roar of effort, Shane Howard's body tensed and Wendy found herself feeling momentarily weightless as her feet left the ground and she felt herself moving uncontrollably towards the road. Trying to regain her footing and stop the forward momentum with her hands on the sharp, gritty surface of the road, she twisted over on her ankle, a pain which was dominant only momentarily before the sharp, searing crunch of her lower back put an end to all forward momentum with a screeching of tyres.

She found herself looking at the front of the Volvo from an unnaturally low position, her back howling with pain as she lost all concept of space and time.

32

Wendy groaned as she came round to find herself in Mildenheath General Hospital once again. The pain had dulled, she noticed, as she tried to sit up straight and relieve the uncomfortably stiff feeling she had in her back. She recognised this particular numbness as the beauty of hospital-strength painkillers.

'Good, you're awake. Now get some soup down your neck and tell them you're feeling fine and we can get back out and nick that bastard.'

'Guv. Just the person I like to see when I wake up,' Wendy said, attempting to smile.

'You're one of few women to have the pleasure, Knight. How you feeling?'

'I must say I've been better.'

'You've been worse, too.'

The whistling of no particular song increased in volume as the white door swung open and the smiling doctor introduced himself in a deep Scottish brogue.

'Ah, Wendy. Doctor Fraser. I think I'm probably more familiar with you than you are with me, after the past couple of hours. You've had a bit of a nasty accident. Do you remember much about it?'

'I remember bouncing off a Volvo.'

'Aye, you tried attacking it with your spine. Not the best weapon the human body has,' Dr Fraser chuckled, his lilting Scottish tones acting as a natural painkiller for Wendy.

'So when can I get out of here?' she asked.

'When you're better, Wendy. You've had a nasty accident and we're still waiting on some test results to make sure nothing is broken or seriously damaged. We're pretty sure it's just bruising, but better safe than sorry.'

The thought had lingered anonymously at the back of Wendy's mind. Now it raced to the front, shouting and screaming.

'And what about... what... did you do scans?'

Dr Fraser glanced sideways at DCI Culverhouse, then back towards Wendy.

'It's OK. He knows,' she said.

'Well, yes. We did,' the doctor said. 'You knew you were pregnant?'

'Yeah, I did. Hang on, what do you mean by were?'

'Wendy, you suffered quite a nasty fall.'

'I know that. What's happened to my baby?'

A thousand thoughts raced through her mind, a ten-thousand-volt surge of adrenaline made her heart heavy with pain.

'I'm so sorry, Wendy.'

Dr Fraser's eyes lowered with sorrow as Culverhouse squeezed Wendy's hand. A choking sob was all she could manage.

33

The only thing to overwhelm her feeling of grief was that of shame. Wendy had lived through the pain of losing both her mother and her father as well as her lover in the space of a few years, and here she was mourning an unborn baby. A foetus. An embryo. A biological organism. It had no name and it had no life, but she found herself grieving harder than she could ever have expected.

It had no form and it had no gender, but Wendy felt overwhelmed at the loss of what she saw as her little girl. It had always been a girl. Deep down, she knew that.

She could not shake the invasive, destructive feeling that it was her body that had killed the baby. If not her body, then her brain. Her stupidity. Just one foolish moment could end it all. A life which had no chance to flourish. A girl who had no chance to get married. A child who had no chance to have a mother. In more ways than one, she felt utterly empty.

Wendy thought back to her childhood. The times when she was happy. The times she had desperately wanted her child to have. A loving parent who epitomised the perfect role model. That was what she had had, and that was all she had ever wanted to be for her child. Those long, never-ending summers spent building tree-houses and dens, all concept of time lost in the innocence and pure unbounded joy of divine youth. All of these things that she had had and wanted her child to have. The child that would never have them. The child that would never even know it had existed.

For the first time since the day before, Wendy responded to the doorbell. She knew it would be Jack.

On opening the door to see him stood there with a large bouquet of lilies and a sorrowful look on his face, she crumbled and sobbed heavily into the crook of his shoulder. For Culverhouse, this was an uncomfortable situation in so many ways.

'I... I don't know what to say.'

'That doesn't usually stop you,' Wendy remarked, in an attempt to maintain some normality, as though playing up to the character she knew she was. In real life. On any other day. In a world where her baby wasn't dead.

'How do you feel?' Culverhouse asked, at a loss for anything more prophetic to say.

'I don't know. I really don't know.'

'Did they... did they say anything about it?'

'There's nothing they can say,' Wendy almost whispered as she stared through red, tear-tinted eyes at the glass-panelled back door. 'But I know it was a girl.'

'Oh. Did you...'

'Have a name for her? I didn't. But I do now.'

Culverhouse cocked his head to the side in anticipation of the answer.

'Roberta. She would've been my little Bobbi.'

34

The latch clicked shut gracefully, Jack allowing his body weight to sink into the door as he exhaled deeply. He wasn't particularly good in these sorts of situations. He knew that. He found it difficult to be the loving, caring shoulder to cry on. Ironically, that made it even harder and more emotionally draining for Jack Culverhouse, a man without emotion.

Pain and emotion are like drugs. The body becomes immune after a while. When one has felt deep pain and anguish, the threshold rises. Jack's immunity to emotion had risen to the point where he wasn't sure he could feel pain any more. His heart told him otherwise.

Inside, deep down, it still hurt incredibly. The worst part was not knowing where they were and whether or not they were alive. He'd dealt with thousands of missing people and runaway wives in the course of his career and he knew they'd be living the high life on a beach resort on the Costa Del Sol, in all probability, but that made it no easier. There was always that deep, dark, lingering thought. Sometimes, he had hoped she wasn't alive. At least it would mean she wasn't enjoying herself.

Tonight was one of those nights where he didn't want to go to sleep. Sleep meant trying to sleep. Trying to sleep meant thinking. Thinking meant hurting. If he stayed up he'd be tired, but at least he wouldn't be lying alone in the dark, alone with his thoughts.

Reading was his escape. An escape to a world where the bad guys always got caught and the good guys always won. An escape to a world that didn't exist. An escape to pure fantasy. It also kept his mind busy and stopped him thinking of things he didn't want to think about.

Once inside the kitchen, he pulled the coffee pot from the back of the cupboard and rummaged in the larder for filter papers and ground coffee. It was rare that his eyes even caught the gaze of most of these shelves. He knew there must be tins and jars that were years past their sell-by date, but he couldn't bring himself to go through the whole lot looking for piddly little sell-by dates on the packets. He never ate any of that shit anyway. Eggs and bread could go a long way for a single man.

The kettle boiled and the coffee filtered, Jack sat down in his living-room armchair with a copy of Ian Rankin's *Knots and Crosses*. He liked Rebus. He'd already read the series through once, but he'd enjoyed it enough to go through again. Although the books were eerily reminiscent of what he faced every day at work, it was still escapism.

Within ten minutes he had fallen asleep, his mind drifting into pleasant dreams, his mug of coffee slowly going cold.

35

The ringing of the office phone went unanswered for four and a half rings before Culverhouse picked up the receiver.

'What?' he barked.

'It's Jackie on the front desk, Inspector. Uniform have just picked up someone who you've got a request out for. A Shane Howard. He's been taken in for shoplifting and we were about to let him go until we saw the note on the system. He's in a holding cell waiting for you.'

'Right. I'll be straight down.'

Culverhouse couldn't stop the smile from spreading on his face as he palmed open both of the double-doors to the custody suite and left them akimbo, as if to welcome an old friend.

'Ah! Shane Howard, we meet again!'

'Fuck off, Culverhouse.'

'Now now, Mr Howard. We're in my building now so we'll play by my rules. My friend here says you've been a bit of a naughty boy, so we're going to have to take you down to one of the interview rooms and find out what you know about a few other things we've got bugging us.'

'I ain't tellin' you nuffin'.'

'And if you'd bothered to turn up to school today, you'd know that you've just agreed to tell me everything.' Culverhouse kept talking over the top of Shane Howard's noisy protestations. 'Jackie, can you call DS Knight down here for me, please? I think she'd like to have a word with Mr Howard as well.'

The atmosphere was a mix of nervousness and excitement as a still-smiling Culverhouse sat opposite a defiant Shane Howard, both of whom were waiting for the appearance of DS Wendy Knight. Culverhouse had deliberately picked the one interview suite which had not yet had a camera installed in it. It was mainly used for speaking to people not under caution, but he wasn't one to worry about formalities right now.

Moments later, she entered the room and sat down, not making eye contact with Shane Howard or DCI Culverhouse. Yet again, she had refused to take any more time off work than was necessary, and was back at her desk less than twenty-four hours after being taken to hospital.

'This interview begins at 11.26. Present are Mr Shane Howard; myself, DCI Jack Culverhouse; and DS Wendy Knight. Mr Howard has declined to have a solicitor present. Now, Mr Howard. You told us the other day that you knew Danielle Levy.'

Silence.

'You told us that you admitted having sexual intercourse with her and that you weren't surprised or shocked to find out that she had died.'

Silence.

'Do you have anything to say, Howard?'

Silence.

'Right. Well I don't see any point in carrying on this interview if you're not going to tell us anything. We'll put you in one of our honeymoon suites until we've decided what to do with you. Interview terminated at 11.27. Thank you, DS Knight. You may return to your duties.

I'll see you back upstairs.' Jack Culverhouse spoke calmly and with a slightly over-egged air of propriety.

As the door clicked shut behind Wendy, Culverhouse rose to his feet and lifted Shane Howard off his chair by the collar of his polo shirt and pinned him against the wall, his snarling face reddening and projecting spittle at Shane Howard as he blustered just centimetres away from his face.

'Right, you snivelling little shit. You're going to talk, and you're going to fucking talk good. Your actions the other day not only injured one of my best police officers, but killed an unborn baby. By rights, and in any other civilised country, I'd be shovelling six feet of pig shit on top of your rotting corpse. Unfortunately for me, the only corpses I have are those of a seventeen-year-old girl, a family man and an unborn baby. Now, you are going to tell me every little fucking thing you know about Danielle Levy.'

'I ... I already told you everythin' I know!'

'Bullshit,' Culverhouse grumbled calmly, before delivering a blow to Shane Howard's stomach. Instinctively, his body began to curl before Culverhouse once again pinned him back against the wall.

'Let's try again. Tell me everything about Danielle Levy.'

Culverhouse had the grace to allow Shane Howard a few moments to regain his breath.

'All right. All right. Like I told you, I just shagged her a few times. It were nothing special, like. Just the usual, you know.'

'So who killed her?'

'How the fuck should I know?'

Culverhouse's face grew redder, his teeth beginning to bare.

'All right! I swear, I don't know! She weren't the kind of girl to have enemies, so I really don't know. I mean, there was girls at school what didn't like her as much as others, but nothing special, y'know? No-one who'd want to kill her, like.'

'Does the name Gary McCann mean anything to you?'

'McCann? Yeah, course it does. Why?'

'Tell me what you know about McCann.'

'Not much.'

Another blow to the stomach.

'Jesus fucking Christ! I told you, I don't fucking know him! Everyone knows who he is and that, but I don't know him personal, like. He's got a place on Meadow Hill Lane. Runs a few businesses. Nasty piece of work, apparently.'

'Did he know Danielle Levy?'

'I dunno, I doubt it. She might have worked in one of his pubs or something. I swear, I really didn't know her all that well.'

Culverhouse let go of Shane Howard and walked back towards the door.

'You're not the only one. The more I find out about Danielle Levy, the less I know.'

36

Wendy found herself sat in the waiting room at the counsellor's office once again. The counsellor she told herself she didn't need. The counsellor who spoke nothing but the truth. The counsellor who could now give her hope in her hour of need.

The room felt colder than before in so many ways. The whole world seemed cold now. Cold and empty, like her womb. She wasn't sure what she wanted and she wasn't sure what she was going to say, but she knew she needed to be here, needed to speak to someone who might understand. No-one would really understand, but Linda Street could try. Maybe condescension was what she needed. Something to ground her again.

Linda Street's office no longer looked warm and welcoming. The soft, fluffy toys were as cold as ice, and the cosy, plump chairs were as hard as steel. For a fleeting moment, she wondered whether anything would ever feel the same again.

Linda's voice was soothing and understanding. More so than normal.

'Wendy, what you've been through is extremely traumatic. The brain is a wonderful tool and it can cope admirably with many situations. The problem is, it's almost impossible to tell when it isn't coping until it's too late.'

'So you're trying to tell me I'm about to go mental?'

'I'm trying to tell you the brain is as fragile as it is wonderful. I don't know anyone who has had to go through the trauma you have in such a short space of time. Talking through these incidents will help your brain to deal with them and heal itself more quickly.'

'My brain isn't broken,' Wendy said quietly but confidently.

'There's no telling what hidden damage has been done, Wendy. What do you have to lose?'

What do I have to lose? Fuck all. I've already lost it all.

Linda Street nodded and smiled at Wendy's silent acceptance, as if she knew what she was thinking.

'What do you feel, Wendy?'

'Nothing.'

'You must feel something. Do you remember the last time you came to see me? All those words you gave me to describe your mixed emotions?'

'Yes. And now I feel nothing.'

'Hurt?'

'No.'

'Dirty?'

'No.'

'Angry?'

'No.'

Linda Street paused for a moment.

'Empty?'

Wendy matched her pause.

'No.'

She knew this was a double-edged sword. Physically, of course, she was empty. Barely hours earlier she had been carrying her unborn child — her hopes, her future. Now she was carrying nothing but grief.

'Wendy, I really do think it would be beneficial for you to take some time off work.'

'I told you before, I don't do time off work. I don't do moping, I don't do daytime TV and I don't do rest. Work takes my mind off things just fine, thank you.'

'Do you not think work is a little too close to what has happened?'

'I'm sorry, but my job is a little different to yours.

You might be happy sat in your little office with your stuffed toys, being all perceptive by telling people that they're upset because bad things have happened to them, but my job isn't quite like that. I catch killers, Dr Street. Do you not understand that? If I don't work, people die.'

'I understand perfectly, Wendy, but I just think that—'

'Oh, you think nothing! You don't need to think! I wish I had that luxury, but unfortunately I don't.'

'Wendy, I just—'

'Save it, doctor. The session's over.'

37

DCI Culverhouse was incredulous at the slow progress of the investigation. Two bodies, one possible link to a cold case and two potential suspects. The only problem was that Gary McCann had, at best, a very weak motive for wanting Danielle Levy dead and Shane Howard had no reason to want to kill Bob Arthurs. He was sure, absolutely convinced, that the two must be connected somehow. The same MO, the same hallmarks, the same small town within hours of each other.

In Culverhouse's experience, it was extremely unlikely that the two murders could have been committed by two different people. Even if they had worked in tandem, or with some sort of connection, the likelihood of that happening was quickly approaching zero.

As he lay back on his sofa and closed his eyes, he tried to clear his mind of all extraneous noise and find some sort of purchase on his thoughts.

No fingerprints, no DNA evidence, and nothing to tell the families of the two victims. As much as Culverhouse cared little for the human race in general, he hated — absolutely loathed — not being able to give families closure and explain who had killed their loved ones and why. He knew how it felt to need answers and not have any.

* * *

This was it. This was the place she'd been told. She meandered up the short driveway, skirting the edge of the lawn, careful to avoid crunching the gravel underfoot with her heels. Being heard would do her no good.

When she had reached the front door, she stepped lightly onto the terracotta tiles and listened carefully, her ear pressed against the door. The only sound, and one which made her heart momentarily jump, was the sound of front door banging shut across the street. She stepped back behind the conifer to make sure she wouldn't be seen.

There was no other sound. She tip-toed around to the front of the bay window and glanced furtively around the edge of the curtain. She had to position herself more perpendicularly than she would have liked, but she had to see for herself. The concrete felt cold through her shoes, hardening with every moment.

As she peered in through the bay window, she could see him there, hands lain across his chest, which heaved with every breath. Good, his eyes were closed. She could take a few moments longer. She crouched down and watched. Just watched. It was definitely Jack. And he had aged.

38

It was becoming all too common an occurrence for DS Knight and DCI Culverhouse to be visiting 101 Heathcote Road. The home of Danielle Levy had never quite had the same warm, welcoming feel as most houses, especially since her disappearance and subsequent death. The pair were grateful for the opportunity, however, to speak to Miriam Levy alone in the absence of her partner.

'Mrs Levy, we appreciate how hard this must be for you, but we believe we may have some clues which may lead us to Danielle's killer. We just need to ask you a few questions, is that all right?'

Wendy was respected throughout the force for her ability to speak calmly and with respect to bereaved families. It was never easy, but she had always been a natural at it. 'Do you know of a man called Gary McCann?'

'Umm... no, I don't think so,' Miriam replied, her voice almost a whisper.

'Do you know if your daughter might have known him?'

'I don't know. Danielle was very open with us, but she didn't tell us about everyone she knew.'

It struck Wendy that Miriam Levy was a woman of few words, a woman whose natural beauty and youthful looks had given her more than words ever could.

'Do you know if she had an address book or anywhere she might have kept a list of people she knew? Contacts, I mean.'

'Maybe her mobile phone. That's all I can think of.'

'Ah. Well we've not been able to retrieve that yet. Is there anywhere else? Did she back up her phone anywhere?'

'I don't know. I don't think so. I wouldn't know how.'

The closing of the front door startled the three of them at once as Darren Parker entered the living room.

'Hello again. Can I help?'

'Ah, Mr Parker,' Culverhouse said, standing to shake Darren's hand. 'We were just speaking to your wife about a possible lead we have in finding Danielle's killer. Tell me, do you know a Gary McCann at all?'

'Gary McCann? Well, yes, of course,' Darren said.

Wendy and Culverhouse glanced at each other, then back at Darren Parker.

'How?' Wendy asked.

'Well, he owns the Spitfire pub. The building, anyway. Someone else is the licensee. He's got a few in the town as well.'

'And what relevance does this have to Danielle?'

Darren Parker looked at Miriam before continuing.

'Well, she had a part-time job there. Glass collecting, mainly, and a bit of bar work as well. I mean, she wasn't far off eighteen and it doesn't really matter too much out of the town centre, does it?'

'When was this, Mr Parker?' Wendy asked.

'Few weeks ago now. There was a disagreement and Danielle stopped working there.'

'What kind of disagreement?'

'Well, it's all a bit complicated, really.' Darren Parker sat down in the armchair by the large bay window. 'There'd been some money going missing from the till. Danielle and a couple of the other girls were on cash-in-hand, you know, and used to get a few tips and things from some of the old men but Gary McCann was sure someone was nicking from him. Reckons stuff was going missing from the safe at one point, too. For some reason he thought it was Danielle and that was that.'

'He sacked her?'

'Yeah, pretty much. Said he didn't want her in there again.'

'And how did Danielle react to that?'

'Well, she was livid. She wouldn't do anything like that in a million years.'

'Did she say that she was going to take any action?'

'Well, no. Not in so many words.'

'Not in so many words? Why? What did she say, Mr Parker?'

'Nothing. Not really. Just one of those heat of the moment things, you know. Silly, really.'

'What did she say?' Culverhouse repeated, this time more forcefully than Wendy had.

Darren Parker sighed.

'She said she was going to make sure he regretted it.'

39

Outside the interview room, the tension was rising.

'We've only got a couple of hours, then we've got to charge him or let him go,' Wendy said.

'I'm perfectly aware of how the policing process works, thank you, Detective Sergeant Knight. Now, if you'll stop wasting my fucking time we can use some of those precious moments to interview the cocky, shit-headed—' Wendy opened the door to the interview suite. '—lovely, adorable Gary McCann.'

McCann looked up at him, unsure of quite how to react.

'Just one of my ways of calming down before an interview, Mr McCann. A bit like the old trick of imagining the other person naked, but I use this one for the fatties.'

The pair took their seats and Wendy switched the tape machine to "record" before Culverhouse stated the legalities.

'Right. We've just been round to speak to Danielle Levy's step-dad, and he tells me you did know Danielle,' Culverhouse continued.

'Well he's lying, ain't he?'

'Doesn't seem like it. He had quite a detailed story, actually. Said she used to work in one of your pubs and got the sack for nicking stuff. Ring any bells?'

'Not especially. I've got a lot of pubs and a lot of businesses. People get fired every day. Way of the world, ain't it?'

'Well maybe this will ring a bell. For the benefit of the tape, I am showing Mr McCann a photograph of Danielle Levy.'

Gary McCann shook his head. 'Nope. Like I said, I've got loads of girls working for me in my pubs. Don't even meet most of them. Just come and work for a few weeks then they're off again. It ain't exactly a job that demands company loyalty, Inspector.'

'So you're saying that you don't remember employing or terminating the employment of Danielle Levy in the last few weeks?'

'Like I said, Inspector. I've got a lot of girls working

for me. I don't know all their names. Besides, it's the licensees who manage staffing in the pubs.'

Culverhouse felt sure he knew differently.

'Surely your payroll system would be able to shed some light on it?'

'Don't have one. Pay them all in cash, don't I?'

'Surely you need a payroll system for National Insurance contributions,' Wendy added.

'Nope. All my bar staff work part time hours. Don't earn enough to pay no National Insurance.'

'Well, aren't you a responsible employer,' Culverhouse said sarcastically.

'Nothing illegal about it, Inspector. Anyway, are you questioning me for murder or money laundering?'

'I think it's best to concentrate on them one at a time, don't you? Now, Danielle Levy's step-dad tells us that Danielle made some sort of remark about "getting you back". Does that ring any bells?'

'Said what, to me?'

'No, to her step-father.'

'Then how the fuck should I know? I don't have microphones in their fucking house. Look, what is this? Are you going to charge me with this girl's murder or let me go? You're running out of time, Inspector.'

'Oh, I have all the time in the world, McCann. Now, tell me, what could a seventeen-year-old girl possibly

have on you which would make you want to see her
dead?'

Before Gary McCann could even formulate an
answer, the knock on the door broke the uncomfortable
silence. Pausing for a few moments and barely breaking
eye contact with McCann, Culverhouse commanded
the knocker to enter. It was Luke Baxter. He gestured
for Culverhouse to leave the interview room for a
moment.

'Guv, we've just had a call from someone. Reckons
he might have some information which connects Bob
Arthurs and Danielle Levy.'

40

Jack Culverhouse felt more than dishevelled as he knocked on the door of Shaun Jackson's house. It was no time to be called out to interview potential witnesses. Especially not people who'd probably turn out to just be another crank. He swore to himself that he'd have Luke Baxter's knackers in a vice if this one turned out to be a crank as well.

The front door clicked open to reveal a well-built man who appeared to be in his early forties. A tradesman, he presumed. Culverhouse prided himself on being able to tell what sort of person someone was purely based on looks. A copper's instinct, perhaps. Satisfied with his brief summing up, Culverhouse introduced himself and was welcomed into the house, carefully stepping around the St Bernard dog which had barked to signal his arrival.

'Nice dog. What's her name?'

'Holly,' the man replied.

Culverhouse's bullshit machine was in full swing. He hated dogs. He also hated the noise of games consoles in the background as he tried to speak to witnesses. Fortunately for him, Shaun had picked up on this.

'Aaron, will you pack that in? Go and play upstairs with Hannah or something, will you?'

The blonde-haired teenager grunted as he switched off the X-Box and trundled off upstairs.

'So. You told one of our officers that you had some information for us?' Culverhouse said.

'Yes, well, I'm not sure if it'll be much use to you, but I think I have something which might connect Danielle Levy and Bob Arthurs.'

Culverhouse's eyes lit up.

'Well, I say a link between Danielle Levy and Bob Arthurs,' he continued. 'I mean more of a link between Miriam Levy and Bob Arthurs.'

'Go on...' Culverhouse's patience was wearing thin.

'Well, it's probably none of my business to say, but I've been a friend of Sylvia Arthurs for quite some time now.

She used to work for my kitchen fitting business. Miriam Levy is a very perceptive woman, but she's also a very loyal woman. The fact of the matter is that Sylvia had known for some time that Bob was... well, playing around, let's say. She had found text messages and overheard phone calls. The woman he was seeing was Miriam Levy.'

'So you're saying that Bob Arthurs was killed by his wife?'

'I don't imagine so, Inspector, no. The funny thing is, Sylvia mentioned to me not long before Bob's death that her solicitor had been in contact regarding the amendment to his will. Sylvia knew nothing about it, other than that Bob had obviously made some changes. Now, I'm no detective, but I suppose that leaves you with four real suspects. Sylvia Arthurs, Miriam Levy, Darren Parker and Danielle Levy.'

'Danielle Levy? So you're saying her death was some sort of revenge, or what?'

'I'm just telling you what I know. The rest is up to you, Inspector.'

Having said his goodbyes to Shaun Jackson, Culverhouse went over the list again.

Sylvia Arthurs. Had found out that her husband had

been having an affair with a younger woman and bumped him off.

Miriam Levy. As the lover, it was quite possible that Bob Arthurs had changed his will to include her as a beneficiary to his estate. Did she kill him to get his money?

Darren Parker. As the long-term partner of Miriam Levy, did he kill Bob Arthurs in a fit of rage?

Danielle Levy. Other than the threat to her mother and step-father's relationship, she had no reason to want Bob Arthurs dead. And, for some reason, she was now dead too.

41

The house at 101 Heathcote Road appeared to be reverting to some sort of sense of normality as DCI Culverhouse inspected the photographs on the mantelpiece for the umpteenth time that week.

'Mrs Levy, I know you're going through a lot with your daughter, but I need to ask you a question about a case which may be linked. Did you know a Bob Arthurs?' he asked.

Miriam Levy's eyes darted to the side, her chest visibly shuddering at the sudden intake of breath.

'Mrs Levy? Did you know Bob Arthurs?'

'I ... Yes. I did.'

'I need to ask this question, I'm afraid. Were you having an affair with Bob Arthurs?'

Miriam's eyes shot towards Darren Parker, who nodded at her, only just perceptibly. She turned her head back and lowered her chin towards her chest.

'Yes. Yes, I was.'

'Thank you, Mrs Levy. Being open and honest is by far the best way to deal with these things. I just wish you'd mentioned something earlier. Now, do you know of anyone who would want to see Bob Arthurs dead?'

'No. I mean... Well, no.'

'Mr Parker, you knew about the affair?' Culverhouse asked, turning to address Darren.

'Yes. Well, only since he died. Miriam told me everything.'

'And you had no reason to want Bob Arthurs dead?'

'Of course! I had every bloody reason. Only problem is, he was already dead by the time I knew what had been going on.'

'I see. This is an awkward question, Mr Parker. Mrs Levy. But do you know of any reason why Danielle would want to kill Bob Arthurs?'

'God, no!' Darren Parker bellowed. 'My step-daughter is lying in a cold, shallow grave and all you can do is accuse her of murder?'

'I'm not accusing anyone of anything, Mr Parker. I'm trying to find out who killed Bob Arthurs and who killed Danielle Levy.'

'Well you'll not get any closer to the truth by hunting around here,' Miriam Levy said quietly, as if trying to tell Culverhouse something.

Nodding gently, Culverhouse made his excuses and left the house.

42

Sylvia Arthurs sat, disconsolate, sobbing into a handful of tissues as Wendy began to broach the important subject.

'Mrs Arthurs, I realise this must be hard for you, but I need to ask you some awkward questions.'

Silence.

'Were you aware of your husband engaging in extra-marital affairs?'

Still silence.

'Mrs Arthurs. Had Bob been having an affair with Miriam Levy?'

Sylvia Arthurs began sobbing again before finally speaking..

'I had always known. It had been going on for months, if not years. I just didn't know what to do.'

'Were you aware that Bob had changed his will?' Wendy asked.

'Yes,' Sylvia replied, quietly. 'I received a call from the solicitor who wanted me to pass on a message about it being witnessed. I... I didn't know what to say.'

'How did that make you feel?'

'It ripped the heart out of me. I once had a loving husband, and now I had a cheating, lying, failure of an ex-businessman. How do you think it made me feel?'

Wendy paused for a moment, waiting for the right time to ask the question.

'Mrs Arthurs, did you kill your husband?'

'No. Not directly.'

'Not directly?'

Sylvia Arthurs sighed heavily. 'What's the use? You'll find out the truth one day. I ... I paid to have him... removed.'

'You paid? A hit-man?'

'A friend.'

'Which friend?' Wendy asked.

'I can't say. I won't say. Please, Sergeant, just arrest me.'

'How much did you pay him, Mrs Arthurs?'

Sylvia waited a few moments before speaking. 'Ten thousand pounds.'

A bell rang in Wendy's brain. She glanced at the doorway before pointing in its general direction.

'You mean...'

'The ten thousand pounds in the bag, yes. He gave it back to me. He said that I didn't deserve to be brought into it and that he wanted to see me do all right for myself afterwards.'

'Mrs Arthurs, did you pay Gary McCann to kill your husband?'

'Who? Heavens, no. Like I say, it was a friend.'

'Mrs Arthurs, it's not just your husband who is dead. A seventeen-year-old girl is lying six feet under as well. Tell me who you paid.'

Sylvia Arthurs choked back the tears and opened her mouth.

43

Culverhouse smiled cockily as the door to 101 Heathcote Road swung open. He entered without being
invited.

'Ah, Mrs Levy. Good to see you're both in. If you
don't mind, DS Knight and I have a few things we'd like
to broach with you.'

Culverhouse noticed the suitcases propped against
the far wall.

'Going somewhere, are we?' he asked.

'To Cuba. For a holiday. We need it,' Darren Parker
said. He took a seat.

'I'm not too sure you'll be going anywhere just yet,'
Culverhouse said. 'We've just been speaking to Sylvia
Arthurs, Mr Parker. She has just signed a statement

saying that she paid you ten thousand pounds to see that Bob Arthurs was killed.'

'What? Nonsense! What utter rubbish.'

'Of course, nothing can be proved because you returned it to her, didn't you? And you thought you'd throw us off the scent and in the direction of Gary McCann, the man who had sacked your step-daughter only days before. That's why you wrote "G McC" on the note, wasn't it?'

'Inspector Culverhouse, if that's the best you can do, I'm afraid you're going to have to—'

'Oh, there's more, don't you worry. I also know about your role in the death of Danielle Levy.'

'I beg your pardon! I most certainly did not kill my step-daughter.'

'Oh, no. I quite agree.' Culverhouse rose and walked over the mantelpiece, picking up a photograph and smiling. 'You know, I really don't know how I didn't realise earlier. Your wife had Danielle when she was very young, didn't she, Mr Parker?'

'Yes. She was just fifteen. What's that got to do with anything?'

'Mmm. So that puts her where, Thirty-two?'

'Yes. Just.'

'Would you say Danielle was mature in her looks, Mr Parker?'

'I don't know. I suppose so.'

Culverhouse laughed. 'I knew it all along, I think, but it only made itself clear when we were speaking to Sylvia Arthurs. It was the mention of a younger woman that did it for me. Mr Parker, you didn't kill Danielle Levy, did you? You killed your wife, Miriam Levy.'

The woman afore-named as Miriam began to sob uncontrollably.

'And Danielle Levy isn't dead at all, is she? She's sat right here with us. Isn't that right, Danielle?'

She continued to sob.

'Mr Parker, I think you had better tell us everything.'

44

Statement made by Darren Parker at Milden-heath Police Station, witnessed by DCI Jack Culverhouse and DS Wendy Knight.

Ever since I first met Miriam, I had been attracted to Danielle. She was only thirteen when I first met her, I admit. There was a spark. An inexplicable attraction. What does age matter, anyway? I'm not a paedophile. Danielle was sixteen before we had sexual contact of any kind. After the first time, it became regular. Very regular. We had always tried so hard to keep it a secret. I used to come home from work early or we'd meet in secret locations. It was far from ideal, but it's all we had. Through it all, I loved Miriam. You must believe that.

It was only recently that Miriam found out what had been going on. That Friday lunchtime, I was home already. I was in the garden when Danielle came home. We were so stupid. It was just one of those things. We were having sex in the living room and Miriam came home early. We heard the door unlock and both scrambled to get dressed and look innocent like a bad scene from a film. It was too late, though. She had worked out what was going on. That's when all hell broke loose.

There was a scuffle and Miriam ended up tripping over. I can still hear the crack her skull made as it hit the marble mantelpiece. There was no blood; that's the funniest thing. It was as if someone had just flipped the switch. I don't know why, but my first instinct was to make sure she was dead. We dragged her out into the garage and I laid her body on some polythene sheeting and slit her throat with a razor blade. It was as if I hadn't done anything. The blood barely trickled. Even so, I needed to... I needed to make sure she was dead. So I brought the sledgehammer down on her head. You'll find it at the bottom of Sharplow Lake. We didn't know what to do, but I knew we had to get rid of the body.

It was Danielle's idea for her to take on Miriam's identity. They both looked incredibly alike, but Miriam's hair was shorter. Once she wore her make-up and clothes, you could barely tell the difference. We even managed to fool our new neighbours, although they'd only met her a handful of times. It was easy enough to pass it off with a new haircut. We didn't think the body would be found, but we left Danielle's belongings nearby just in case.

It was when the family said they'd come down for the funeral that we started to panic. That's when we decided we would go abroad. We planned to start a new life together.

I had known for a few weeks about Miriam and Bob Arthurs. If the truth be told, the bug had bitten. Death is addictive. It was me who killed Bob Arthurs and poured the acid on his body. I used a baseball bat on him first, then took him to the unit and got him to open it up and give me the alarm code. When we were inside, I hit him again. He was still alive when I began to pour the acid. It was only then that I had the idea of doing the same to Miriam's body, just in case it could still be identified. We dissolved the limbs and head first. They took an absolute age. It was like watching her dying all over again.

When the officers came round and asked for Danielle's hairbrush and an item of clothing, I gave them Miriam's. That's why the DNA matched the body. When the body was identified as Danielle's, we thought we were home and dry. I covered my tracks by making it seems as though Gary McCann was responsible for both murders. I wanted that bastard to hang for what he did to Danielle.

Everyone knows he killed his wife. A criminal is a criminal, and he deserved to go down for murder, not me.

It was me who planted Danielle's hairs in Gary McCann's house and car. I had been fitting a carpet in his dining room and living room and had the perfect opportunity. I couldn't believe it when he called me and asked me to do the job. He just got my number out of the paper. I guess he didn't know who I was. I never told him my surname. I knew who he was, though. Stupid bastard even left his car keys hanging by the front door. It was easy. Too easy.

As the cell door slammed shut and the viewing window slid across into the closed position, Darren Parker laid back and closed his eyes.

The cell felt strangely like home. It was cold, dark and hard. Like so many things. Like life itself. He had come to terms with the fact that he would never see Danielle again.

He was a man who regretted very little. What was the point in regret? The past could never be changed. What didn't kill you only made you stronger. Some simple things took an incredible amount of strength.

Calmly, he raised his knee and ran his finger around the back of the sole of his shoe. The blade slipped out easily and he began to run it between his fingers. With one last breath he raised his head and brought the blade across his throat.

* * *

The pleasant swirling and deep comfort gave way to the rotten stench of real life as the sound of the doorbell woke Culverhouse from his slumber.

As though opening them underwater, he blinked and batted his eyes in an attempt to focus through the slumberous fluid which coated his eyeballs. Groaning half in mock-annoyance, he pushed himself up from the sofa and arched his back before rising to answer the door.

He glanced at his watch. 12:05. Five past midnight. Considering some choice pleasantries with which to furnish his unwelcome late-night visitor, Culverhouse swept aside the chain and pulled open the door.

'Hello, Jack.'

KNIGHT & CULVERHOUSE RETURN IN JACK BE NIMBLE, OUT NOW

As DCI Jack Culverhouse comes to terms with his ex-wife's dramatic return after she disappeared eight and a half years earlier and DS Wendy Knight tries to cope with with the devastating events of two previous cases, a killer is loose on the streets of Mildenheath.

As the body count begins to rise, Knight and Culverhouse start to realise that the killer is emulating the gruesome, grisly murders of the world's most famous and elusive serial killer, Jack the Ripper.

They know he's going to kill again, but they don't know where or who his next victim will be. And what's worse, they don't know who he is either...

Turn the page to read the first chapter...

JACK BE NIMBLE, CHAPTER 1

It felt odd punching an unconscious woman. Wrong, almost. Almost. The tranquilliser wouldn't be wearing off for some time yet, so he had plenty of time to revel in the rollercoaster of emotions.

He steadied himself by leaning forward on the edge of the bathtub, the plastic wrap crunching and rustling as he did so. He had a sudden urge to spit in her face, but knew he had to control himself. Leaving his DNA on the body wouldn't be a great start.

It was getting almost unbearably hot inside the beekeeper's suit but he couldn't remove anything until it was all over. It just wasn't worth the risk.

He pulled the knife out of its leather sheath and turned it in his hand, the light glistening off the steel and bouncing around the room. He pulled it under his nostrils and sniffed. It smelt of nothing — perhaps faintly of leather — but it wasn't the smell he was interested in. It was the sensation.

He looked down at her body and noticed a red mark already appearing where he'd punched her. All he needed to do now was wait until a bruise had started to develop. He couldn't kill her before then, as much as he desperately wanted to. He was fighting the urge with every fibre of his being. He didn't know whether it was excitement, joy or extreme anxiety. Right now he knew only one thing: he had to stick to the plan.

Going off track now could be disastrous. Every minuscule aspect of this had to be carried out to a T. For every stage, he'd even worked out a secondary and, in most cases, a tertiary option should unforeseen circumstances arise. Because unforeseen circumstances always arose.

The only thing he could not be sure of were the exact timings, but that didn't matter too much. The plan he was working from didn't have exact timings. He knew that the red mark on her face would build slightly and some swelling would occur. With any luck, he'd have cracked her cheekbone or caused tissue damage which would be spotted anyway. He wasn't waiting for a full-on purple shiner — that could take days. No, just a nice red welt would do. Enough for them to spot it.

Cutting through her neck hadn't felt at all like he had expected it to. It was like slicing a tough, stringy chicken breast. Even with his ultra-sharp knife he had to rock the knife and work with it to get the effect he wanted. Before long he was almost down to the vertebrae. He'd placed a plastic screen over her upper body and was now struggling to see through it, such was the amount of blood that'd hit it. This job needed to be clean, though, because they couldn't catch him. Not just yet. Not until he was ready.

He carefully peeled back the plastic glove over his left wrist to look at his watch. It was almost time.

Want to read on?

Visit   adamcroft.net/book/jack-be-nimble/ to grab your copy.

GET MORE OF MY BOOKS FREE!

Thank you for reading *Guilty as Sin*. I hope it was as much fun for you as it was for me writing it.

To say thank you, I'd like to give you some of my books and short stories for FREE. Read on to get yours...

If you enjoyed the book, please do leave a review on Amazon. Reviews mean an awful lot to writers and they help us to find new readers more than almost anything else. It would be very much appreciated.

I love hearing from my readers, too, so please do feel free to get in touch with me. You can contact me via my website, on Twitter @adamcroft and you can 'like' my

Facebook   page   at   http://www.
facebook.com/adamcroftbooks.

Last of all, but certainly not least, I'd like to let you know that members of my VIP Club have access to FREE, exclusive books and short stories which aren't available anywhere else. There's a whole lot more, too, so please join   the   club   (for   free!)   at adamcroft.net/vip-club

For more information, visit my website: adamcroft.net

Printed in March 2021
by Rotomail Italia S.p.A., Vignate (MI) - Italy